PUFFIN BOOKS

THE DINOSAUR INVESTIGATOR'S HANDBOOK

Become a Dinosaur Investigator and find out:

● The best places to look for your dinosaur – and what to do if you find one.

● Everything you need to know about fossils and how to locate them.

● The very latest information, with details of dino websites and organizations for you to join.

● All the theories, investigations (and silly mistakes) made by previous investigators.

● Answers to some really Big Questions – like where did dinosaurs disappear to?

● How to keep on investigating dinosaurs – and come up with your own theories.

What are you waiting for – get investigating!

The Dinosaur Investigator's Handbook

Marc Gascoigne

PUFFIN BOOKS

For Maggie, of course

PUFFIN BOOKS

Published by the Penguin Group
Penguin Books Ltd, 27 Wrights Lane, London W8 5TZ, England
Penguin Books USA Inc., 375 Hudson Street, New York, New York 10014, USA
Penguin Books Australia Ltd, Ringwood, Victoria, Australia
Penguin Books Canada Ltd, 10 Alcorn Avenue, Toronto, Ontario, Canada M4V 3B2
Penguin Books (NZ) Ltd, 182–190 Wairau Road, Auckland 10, New Zealand

Penguin Books Ltd, Registered Offices: Harmondsworth, Middlesex, England

First published 1997
1 3 5 7 9 10 8 6 4 2

All photographs supplied by Salamander Picture Library, the Natural History Museum and the
Mary Evans Picture Library

The moral right of the author has been asserted

Filmset in Monotype Baskerville

Made and printed in England by Clays Ltd, St Ives plc

British Library Cataloguing in Publication Data
A CIP catalogue record for this book is available from the British Library

ISBN 0–140–38784–6

Contents

Dinosaurs Stalk the Earth

Aren't dinosaurs *brilliant*!

Humans love dinosaurs. We're fascinated by these ancient, long-dead creatures. Our culture is full of them. They are the stars of films, television shows and books, and their images are all around us: on t-shirts, toys and posters. Despite their incredibly long, Latin, scientific names, we all manage at a very early age to learn the difference between, say, a Tyrannosaurus rex and a Triceratops.

Spot the Tyrannosaurus rex

Some people say it's because they feed into our imaginations. Our fairy stories are full of dragons and other giant beasts – yet here are creatures that once stalked our planet and that were easily the equal of any princess-scoffing, overgrown crocodile of legend. Other people say it's simpler than that: we're just fascinated by the very thought that an animal could grow larger than a double-decker bus and stomp around quite happily, munching on trees – or sometimes on each other. It's just their very unusual size and appearance that makes us wonder about them so much.

If you stop to think about it for a moment, however, this fascination with dinosaurs is all a bit strange. Look at it this way: have you ever seen a real live dinosaur? Nope, neither have we. All we've ever seen have been reconstructions made by scientists – collections of bones, wired together to make a skeleton, or life-size models built of plaster and resin.

Although dinosaur experts have managed to reconstruct dinosaurs from bones dug up out of the earth, not one dinosaur has survived for us to study in the flesh. Sure, since we have been studying their remains with increasing skill for the past 150 years or so, we humans are beginning to get a pretty good idea as to what they looked like.

But doubts remain. Here's another question: what colour are dinosaurs? Was that 'brown' you said, or 'green' or 'multicoloured'? The simple answer is: we don't know for certain. If all you have is a dinosaur's skeleton, guessing the colour of the skin it came wrapped up in is kind of tricky.

Although we know a fair bit about dinosaurs, there is always more that we could do with finding out. Thankfully, there are plenty of opportunities to do this. Professionals and amateurs alike, the world needs more Dinosaur Investigators!

How to be a Dinosaur Investigator

So, do you fancy the job of searching for dinosaurs? You do? Excellent!

We must be honest and tell you at the outset: it can be hard work, and it may involve quite a bit of scrabbling around on your hands and knees in the dust, but the rewards can be great! Just imagine finding your own brand-new species of dinosaur, having it named after you and everything!

There are two types of dinosaur investigator. First, there are the professionals, the 'palaeontologists' who work for natural history museums the world over. Although these scientists come in a variety of shapes and sizes, they all seem to have a few things in common. First, they know millions and millions of facts about dinosaurs. Never mind that GCSE in Triceratops Studies you were thinking of taking instead of French – these guys have university degrees and PhDs and everything. Imagine how many exams you will have to take to get to such a level. Borrring! The study of dinosaurs is a strict science and, as such, it demands the highest standards of study. There must be scientific methods and set ways of doing things, so that no vital piece of information is ever lost. This sometimes means that the everyday work of a palaeontologist is much less than fun.

Oh, and there's another thing it seems you need

in order to be a professional dinosaur investigator: a beard, and the bigger the better. Don't ask us why; that's just the way it is. If you haven't got a huge, straggly clump of facial fungus growing out of your chin, you might as well forget it.

Palaeontologists collecting the remains of a woolly mammoth near Aveley, Essex. Spot any beards?

Luckily there are always vacancies for amateur dinosaur investigators. In fact, many museums rely on the discoveries made by interested folk who search for fossils just in their spare time, as a hobby. With a few simple pieces of equipment and a good idea about where to look, anyone can go out and discover new fossils of creatures that lived millions of years ago. What's more, we'll tell you exactly how to go about doing just that over the next hundred or so pages.

So, stick to being an amateur. If you get really good, and you're already so brainy that you need a whole pocketful of pens in your shirt pocket to jot down all your brilliant ideas, you may even be able to cross over to doing it full time. Just don't forget about growing that beard.

The D-Files

There are two distinct sides to being a dinosaur investigator, even a purely amateur one like yourself.

On the one hand, there's the 'knee-deep in scorching desert dust in the middle of Outer Mongolia' stuff, your genuine Indiana Jones-with-a-trowel, real-life, actual dinosaur excavating. Oh, all right, if we're going to be honest, there's also the more likely circumstances: the 'spending a nice sunny Sunday afternoon wandering along a rocky beach somewhere, looking for a few small fossils' stuff as well. Actually getting out in the field and scrabbling around in the dirt in search of a few old bones can be great fun, that's for sure – especially if you manage to find something! The best thing about this is that anyone can do this, at least on a small scale. Once you've tried it a few times and seen how easy it is to find fossils, you may find you want to do it all the time.

To be a truly great dinosaur investigator, however, you need to know what you're looking for, where to look for it, and what to do with it when you find it – if you ever do! Most of a dinosaur investigator's time is taken up with assembling data and information, to discover the facts about a particular creature or a new discovery.

For example, in those excellent dinosaur movies, *Jurassic Park* and *The Lost World*, Jeff Goldblum's character is the genuine article, albeit a very idealized, Hollywood version of one. You can't exactly imagine him getting his nice suit dirty; he's far more of a books-and-computer-files type of investigator, a man who's up to date with the latest scientific theories and the newest discoveries.

So here's what you should do: create your own 'Dinosaur Files'. Gather together every scrap of information about dinosaurs and other fossils that you can. Include photographs, drawings and clippings from newspapers and magazines. Also include your own fossils, if you are lucky enough to find any, along with careful records of where and how you found them. Countless new creatures are waiting to be discovered by the lucky dinosaur investigator, and there are a thousand and one unanswered questions to be asked about those we already know. If you are prepared, maybe you will be the person to make the next big breakthrough!

Know your dinosaurs

A keen investigator should be familiar with all the latest theories concerning dinosaurs and their ori-

gins. Obviously you already have the most useful aid
for doing this right here in your hands. To help
expand your investigations, we've also included a
handy section on further reading at the end of this
book. Your local library should be able to help track
down any particularly obscure titles for you to bor-
row.

New information is always being released by
palaeontologists. Barely a week goes by, it seems,
without some fabulous new discovery or theory
being trumpeted on the news and in the papers.
Read as much as you can on the subject, but don't
forget to swot up on mistakes, controversies and
frauds, just as much as on the well-documented
cases. It sounds like hard work, but dinosaur investigators have to be prepared to use their brains. It's all
too easy to jump to conclusions, to think that that
massive bone you've found under your Gran's rose
bush is a genuine Apatosaurus thigh rather than the
old branch it plainly is. Know how other, less expert
people than yourself get fooled, and you won't make
the same mistakes. Will you?

In these days of the Internet, the World Wide
Web and all the other hi-tech malarkey, clued-up
investigators have access to the latest cybernetic ana-
lytical devices. You may be startled to learn that you
do too, if you have a home PC. Keep all your
records on computer files, including details of every
fossil you find for your collection. Look at the files
using a variety of categories: not just date, time and
place, but type of rock, possible creature identifica-

tion, any similarities to other fossils, and any possible explanation there could be for its formation. Look for patterns, so you'll recognize the same thing the next time you see it.

The Internet itself may prove to be a vital resource for many investigators. Because it's not governed by any one group of people, it is home to all kinds of pretty batty arguments and explanations for the big questions – but the truth must be out there somewhere, as someone on the telly once said. If you have a connection at school or at home, keep tuned in to the dinosaur home pages for the latest developments on the World Wide Web. We've surfed the Web (hey, are we cool or what!) to produce a list of hot Web site addresses, and we've included them at the end of this book.

FILE STATUS

As we take you through every aspect of being a dinosaur investigator, you will come across special sections posing the Big Questions that every investigator wants to answer. Big Questions like 'Where on Earth did all those dinosaurs go to, all of a sudden?' As you continue your own investigations, you may be able to solve some of these for yourself! Assemble your Dinosaur Files, gather all the evidence, and who knows what new theories you may come up with?

The Golden Rules

OK, so are you ready to become a fully fledged dinosaur investigator. You are? All right! In that case, you just need to read the small print, in the form of these Golden Rules that you must promise to observe at all times.

Seek out the truth: There are some pretty Big Questions about dinosaurs which still need to be answered (we pose them later in this book). If you're diligent, you may even be able to help answer them yourself. Build your files, gather up all the data, and you'll be in a better position to do just that. Know the facts, but also find out how other, lesser investigators who came before you made silly mistakes.

Fossils are wonderful things to collect. It's a real thrill to find them, as you'll soon discover. But there's a deeper purpose to it all, too. Once you've been collecting your own fossils for a while, you'll come to understand that it's not just finding fossils that's the fun – it's finding that rare, extremely unusual fossil. It may even be a fossil no one else has ever found before. Imagine that!

Be scientific: If you do find a fossil, don't get carried away by the excitement. Ensure that you make notes and take photographs or draw sketches of where it came from. Keep a record of how it was when you found it, what sort of rock it was in, and so on. You never know, there may just come a time when a big, important chap from the Natural

History Museum, complete with extremely bushy beard, will be standing in front of you, asking you to show him exactly where you found that brand-new type of Tyrannosaur's head. If you can't tell him, you're going to look a right twit!

Be really, really careful: This is the most important rule – read this section twice! If you are determined to go off looking for fossils, especially in out-of-the-way places such as an isolated beach or hillside, use your common sense first. Tell someone more responsible than your baby sister where you're going. Better still, rope in an interested grown-up to come along and supervise. Don't ever wander off on a fossil-hunting expedition on your own.

Don't even think about digging anything out of a cliff or hillside unless a responsible adult is present to ensure that it really is safe. Also, you will need to be sure that you are wearing all the right safety gear, typically a safety helmet, goggles and thick gloves. Believe us, nothing spoils an afternoon more than being buried under thousands of tonnes of rock. Stay safe, or you'll end up as extinct as all those dinosaurs.

The very best thing you can do is join your local fossil society or natural history club and take part in a properly organized fossil hunt. Such groups know where it's safe to dig. They may even kit you out with all the right gear and take you to some extra-special fossil sites which are normally off-limits to the general public.

This brings us to the last point. Make certain that you have permission to take fossils away. There are some places where you are not allowed simply to stroll up and pocket all the fossils in sight. Most national parks and other scenic areas won't allow you to dig out fossils; some even ban you from picking them up off the ground. Always make sure that you have permission for a fossil hunt *before* you start stuffing your bags.

What's a Fossil?

What an odd word it is: *fossil*. It's like one of those words you start saying out loud and then totally forget what it means. Try it. Fossil.

It comes from the Latin word *fossilis*, which used to mean 'something dug out of the ground'. Up until the nineteenth century, that could include lumps of coal, bits of old Roman pottery, coins, buried treasure . . . just about anything.

These days, however, the meaning has changed. In general speech, in phrases such as 'you old fossil', the word means something or someone very ancient indeed, old-fashioned and decrepit. For modern dinosaur investigators, however, fossils are far more exciting.

Fossils are the naturally preserved remains of dead creatures. People have been digging them out of the ground or stumbling across them for centuries, but only nowadays can we be certain how they were formed. Fossils can range in size from the tiniest plants and animals, right down to bacteria, all the way up to the gigantic preserved bones of the most enormous dinosaurs.

Fossils are usually solid stone versions of creatures, formed when their bodies were buried and their chemical make-up changed over millions of years. A smaller proportion of fossils have been preserved by other means, such as being trapped in tar, tree-sap, ice, peat, and so on.

Most fossils represent only the hard parts of

creatures, such as their bones, teeth or shells. However, in a few rare cases far softer body-parts have been preserved. Eggs, footprints, skin imprints and even hardened droppings have all come down to us as fossils.

Sad to say, very few fossils that have been discovered are the whole bodies or skeletons of a particular creature. They are far more likely to be just fragments: a few teeth or a single small bone, if you are lucky. Only small sea creatures, from long before the time of the dinosaurs, are commonly found intact. Many more fossils are little more than a glimpse of a creature's passing: the tunnel of a worm through the sand, the mark of a leaf on hardened mud, the preserved footprint of a dinosaur. Possibly the best-known fossils are distinctly dull: coal and oil, which have developed from ancient deposits of wood and plankton respectively. (All right, dull, but the world would be very different without them!)

Over the last 150 years or so, investigators have collected literally millions of fossils. However, that vast total is still tiny compared to the uncountable numbers that remain buried in the earth. Most are too hard to get at, granted – deep under the sea or mountains, under polar ice or thick jungle. Others, however, are just sitting there waiting to be found by someone like you.

OK, so what's a dinosaur?

The most famous and the most fascinating fossils of them all are the remains of dinosaurs, giant reptiles which stalked the Earth until about 65 million years ago.

It is commonly believed that a 'dinosaur' is any animal that is old, stuffy, slow-moving and afraid of change. That's kind of a mistake really because, as we are beginning to realize, some members of the dinosaur family were very youthful and fast-moving indeed. And as for being afraid of change, well, the way that dinosaurs seemed to have evolved quickly lays that one to rest too.

If we're being accurate for a moment (and we are), dinosaurs are actually only one group of a whole range of reptiles that lived before man came on the scene. More than that, alongside the reptiles there were also mammals, fish, insects, spiders, crabs, plants, trees and many more.

Scientifically speaking, the dinosaurs were one branch of the Archosaurs. That's a dinosaur investigator's name for a group of reptile-like creatures that included dinosaurs, pterodactyls, crocodiles and alligators, sea-dwelling creatures like Plesiosaurs, and a number of other, lizard-like beasts. Without wishing to sound too boffin-like, dinosaurs are different from all the rest because of the shape of their hips. These must have swung their legs under their bodies when they moved and have given them an upright, erect posture – compared, say, to the way a crocodile slinks about with its legs sprawled out sideways.

Interestingly, these same hips continue to be found nowadays – in birds. After years of debate, it now seems pretty certain that all the thousands of bird species which share our planet with us are not only descended from dinosaurs, they actually – in scientific terms, at least – are genuine members of the dinosaur family! Thankfully for us, however, there are no seventy-tonne, long-necked, Diplodocus-sized birds around today – which is just as well, as they'd make a terrible mess of your bird-table.

It must be said right from the start that most fossils are not those of dinosaurs. Sorry about that. Fossils of all land animals are comparatively rare. Most creatures that die on the land have their bodies eaten by predators, worms, bacteria, and so on. Bones then decay further in the soil, or are eaten away by the wind and the rain. The formation of any fossil requires a very special set of circumstances, as well shall soon explain. It's actually pretty improbable that there are any fossils still around for us to collect. Whatever, the chances of fossils forming are far greater in the sea than on land and, unfortunately, most dinosaurs did live on the land. Of course, knowing that dinosaur fossils are rare just makes us search even harder to find them.

Swallowed a dictionary?

Since the study of rocks and the fossil remains preserved within them is a proper branch of science, there are a number of long words that we can't avoid using (but we'll put an explanation of them in our special dictionary section at the end of this book).

The first is *palaeontology* (pronounced pay-lee-ontolo-gee). It's the scientific name for the study of fossils, just as biology is the study of living things and geology is the study of rocks. As you might guess from those examples, fossils are studied by a *palaeontologist*. These days this refers to anyone who studies the remains of animals and plants which lived more than 10,000 years ago.

Giants in the Earth

People must have been digging odd-sized bones and solidified creatures out of the ground for thousands of years. However, the serious study of fossils began only about 300 years ago, at the dawn of our modern scientific age. Before that, all kinds of theories were put forward to explain the discovery of what we now know to be fossils.

Historians have found references to 'dragon's bones' that were used as ingredients in medicines in China way in back in the time of the Han Dynasty (206 BC to AD 220). More recently, sixteenth-century Chinese medical books described such bones in greater detail – leaving us in no doubt they were really dinosaur remains! Other traditional medicines call for the use of 'stone swallows', which they call *shiyyen*, that are really fossilized, clam-like shellfish from the Devonian Period. Interestingly, some rare medicines using these ingredients are still occasionally prescribed by practitioners of traditional Chinese medicine. And you thought cough mixture tasted bad!

In Europe in the Middle Ages, alchemists and scholars investigated what they called the *via plastica* or 'plastic force'. This, they thought, was a strange pressure that caused bones buried in the earth to turn to stone. Since many of them believed that the world had been created only in the year 4004 BC, they had little idea of what we now know: that such processes occur over thousands, if not millions, of years.

Ordinary people knew even less about science; their minds were full of biblical stories, legends and folk tales. Around the year 1600, for example, when a quantity of fossilized mammoth tusks was found in Germany, popular opinion had it that they were the genuine horns of dead unicorns!

Similarly, the many ammonites (coiled, snail-like shells of extinct sea-creatures) found on the beach at Whitby in Yorkshire were said to be the remains of snakes that had been turned to stone by the powers of the town's seventh-century abbess, Saint Hilda. For several centuries, local craftsmen busied them-selves carving heads and eyes on to such fossils to make them look more like snakes. The town's coat-of-arms still includes three coiled fossils.

Not everyone was deluded quite so easily. When Leonardo da Vinci studied the subject of fossils in the fifteenth century, he suggested that they were the petrified remains of once-living organisms. However, his views were hotly disputed at the time, and so he kept them to himself, secreted within his diaries, which were not fully published until the middle of the last century.

Early theories

Fossils continued to be studied alongside geology. Finally, in the seventeenth century the Danish natur-alist Niels Stensen (known as Steno) put forward the theory that fossils might be the remains of ancient creatures, and far older than had previously been thought. Once geologists had accepted their great age, new theories were developed to explain how rocks formed.

The first unmistakable reference to actual dinosaur bones was made in 1677 by Robert Plot, the Keeper of the Ashmolean Museum in Oxford – not that he knew what it was he was describing! He wrote about and illustrated the rounded, knobbly knee-end of a huge thigh bone from Megalosaurus, a two-legged dinosaur that is fairly common in Jurassic rocks in southern England. Plot himself thought it was from a giant human, but now we know differently. Sadly, the fossil itself has been lost.

Other naturalists were less convinced by all this newfangled 'science' nonsense. In 1726, the Swiss naturalist Johann Scheuchzer examined an unusual-looking skeleton, which had been dug up in Germany. He declared it to be the fossilized body of a human who had been drowned in Noah's flood. (It was actually a fossilized salamander, about 35 million years old.)

A major development occurred when the French naturalist, Georges Cuvier, noted that many fossils, while plainly from dead species, shared many common characteristics. By studying, say, a modern lizard, you could work out the probable lifestyle of a similar fossil lizard. In fact he did just this, studying the immense jaws of what turned out to be a Mosasaurus, which was found deep in a chalk mine in Holland in 1770. Cuvier practically invented such 'comparative studies', a field that was to become of the greatest importance in the study of dinosaurs.

Around 1800, the British land surveyor William Smith realized that different layers of rock contained different species of fossils. What's more, he worked out that if rocks included the same type of fossils, they were likely to be of the same age. Using this reasoning, he produced the first geological maps showing the distribution of different types of rock around England.

A little later, in 1810, a woman called Mary Anning was making a living selling fossils which she had found in and beneath the cliffs of Lyme Regis, on the south coast of England. These were chiefly ammonites, which are plentiful in the rocks around there, but between 1810 and 1812 she and her brother managed to dig up a complete 'sea-dragon'. She thought it was a crocodile, and she sold it for the princely sum of twenty guineas (£21). It was only later that palaeontologists realized that this was an Ichthyosaur, and it might have been the first complete fossil reptile ever excavated.

The first true investigators

In 1824, naturalists took stock of all these fascinating fossils, and they came to a startling realization: people were digging up giant reptiles of a sort previously unknown to science!

In 1822, a Sussex doctor and amateur geologist called Gideon Mantell was given some strange fossil teeth. They had been found by his wife, Mary, apparently in gravel used for road-building near by. He realized that they must have come from a plant-eating reptile, a creature far larger than any around at that time. The doctor tracked down the source of the gravel to a quarry at Cuckfield, where he found more artefacts. Since the teeth and bones were so similar to those of the (much smaller) iguana, Mantell proposed in 1824 they had come from a beast he called 'Iguanodon'.

At the same time, the eminent English geologist William Buckland published a paper on some bones – a massive lower jaw, a hind leg and a shoulder – from another huge reptile, this time collected at Stonesfield, Oxfordshire, in 1818. In consultation with Georges Cuvier, Buckland decided that they must have come from an immense new form of reptile, more than sixteen metres long. He called the new species Megalosaurus (or 'huge reptile'). Gideon Mantell, meanwhile, was continuing to search for unusual fossils, and in 1833 he turned up the partial skeleton of a peculiar armoured dinosaur, which he called Hylaeosaurus.

The scientific community was abuzz with the news. In museums around the world, naturalists were re-examining their fossils and they realized that these, too, could be from previously unknown reptilian species. Finally, in 1841, Sir Richard Owen gave an address to the annual meeting of the British Association for the Advancement of Science. He declared that, since the three huge British fossil reptiles were so unlike current species, they should be

Sir Richard Owen, who gave us the word 'Dinosaur'

classed as a new type of creature. He proposed that they be called after the Greek words *deinos* (terrible or fierce) and *sauros* (reptile): the Dinosaur.

In America in 1855, the first scientifically documented finds of reptile teeth from two new dinosaurs were made in the desolate state of Montana. In 1858, the partial skeleton of a Hadrosaurus was excavated in New Jersey. Naturalist Joseph Leidy, helping to restore it, realized that it would not have waddled along on all fours like a crocodile, but that it had a far more kangaroo-like posture. At a single stroke of genius, dinosaurs gained their true shape!

Spurred on by the fame which new discoveries were bringing to their fellows, palaeontologists around the world sought out new and more startling species. In 1861, the first example of what was arguably the most fabulous fossil creature ever was found. It was an Archaeopteryx, a definite link between dinosaurs and birds, a feathered but toothed flying creature. The first example, found in particularly fine limestone rocks in Germany, was headless and featherless. However, a second example, recovered in 1877, was split open – to reveal a complete head and the very definite impressions of feathers all over its body!

In April 1878, miners excavating a coal-seam in Bernissart in Belgium cut into a new, clay-filled fissure. Within it they found at least forty complete or partial Iguanodon skeletons. There were so many bones, naturalists were able to reconstruct several dozen complete creatures!

Dinosaur wars!

Just before the announcement of the Bernissart discoveries, an even richer seam of giant dinosaurs was discovered in Colorado, America. In fact, two discoveries were made there at separate sites. As luck would have it, bones from one site were sent to Edward Drinker Cope, a professor at Yale; bones from the other were sent to Othniel C. Marsh at New Jersey. This pair were already deadly rivals, each constantly trying to outdo the other. Now they were in a race to be the first to discover any new dinosaurs.

Teams of explorers hired by Cope and Marsh extended their search to Como Bluff in Wyoming, to Montana, to New Mexico and to the Connecticut Valley. In many places their teams struck dinosaur

Two of the explorers sent by Cope and Marsh make an exciting find in Wyoming, USA

gold. From 1877 to 1890 the pair between them turned up over 130 new species, including Diplodocus, Allosaurus, Apatosaurus (also known as Brontosaurus) and Stegosaurus. However, such finds were often bought at a price. Stories emerged of claim-jumping, of rival teams sabotaging the other's diggings, even of palaeontologists destroying partial fossils so that their rivals could not come afterwards and excavate them.

Dinosaurs everywhere!

At the start of this century, following the deaths of Cope and Marsh, a new attitude to collecting and restoring dinosaur bones took over – thankfully, a far more rigorous and scientific one.

Many famous palaeontological expeditions were sent out in order to find new exhibits for the great museums of the USA, Britain and Germany. Possibly the most famous discoverer was Barnum Brown, whose explorations on behalf of the American Museum of Natural History from 1890 to 1930 took him to the dinosaur fields of Wyoming and Montana. In 1902 Barnum excavated the first Tyrannosaurus rex, at Hell Creek in Montana; in 1908 he found another – no more would be discovered for another fifty years.

At about the same time, the first major Canadian dinosaur discoveries were being made, at Red Deer River, Alberta. This news was quickly followed by another 'dinosaur rush', this time in small boats which had to carry palaeontologists and bones alike across the fetid, mosquito-ridden swamps of the area.

Scientists began to look ever further afield for potential sites. In 1907, large dinosaur remains, including the first Brachiosaurus, were found by German scientists digging at Tendaguru in German East Africa (now Tanzania). The ultimate dinosaur hunt, however, was Roy Chapman Andrews's extremely ambitious expedition to the Flaming Cliffs in Mongolia, from 1922 to 1925. He had actually been looking for the remains of human ancestors but, when his team came across uncountable numbers of dinosaur bones, the expedition hurriedly changed its objective. There, he and his team found many incredible new species: the first Oviraptor, with its toothless, beaked skull; the first Velociraptors, in great numbers. And, finally and most importantly, bones from the previously unknown Protoceratops – and, unbelievably, clutches of eggs from dinosaur nests!

Following the Second World War, several Russian and Polish teams conducted successful expeditions to the same region. From the remotest corners of China came news of major finds, many of which could be seen at an exhibition which toured the world's museums in the 1980s and '90s. Reports of more incredible discoveries from the distant north-west of China started to emerge in May 1997. All round the world, from Argentina to Australia, from South Africa to India, new species of dinosaurs and other large fossil creatures were being excavated and studied.

A new, American-backed expedition returned to Mongolia in 1991–5; it turned up many stunning new skeletons, mainly from previously unknown species (see page 112 for more about their discoveries). The expeditions continue; every year's field season sees amazing new finds.

This is not to say that all new discoveries have to be made by organized teams. The most famous recent dinosaur investigator must be a British amateur, Bill Walker. While digging in a clay pit in Surrey in 1983, he found a spectacular curved claw bone of a size not previously reported. Experts from the Natural History Museum in London soon realized that it was from a brand-new species. They helped him excavate the rest of the creature, a totally new type of fish-eating dinosaur, and they named it Baryonyx walkeri after its discoverer.

How Fossils are Made

So that's how scientists came to understand what fossils are. But where do fossils come from, how are they made? The study of fossilization is called *taphonomy*, and it's carried out by a *taphonomist*. For a few pages, let's assume we're all taphonomists.

As we've already explained, fossilization is the coming together of a number of chance events; most dead creatures and plants are not turned to fossils but merely decay back into the soil. However, when it does occur, fossilization generally involves the replacement of the original body or bones of a creature with other, more solid material that will stay around long after the softer material surrounding it has been worn away. Typically, this occurs when a bone or a tooth is buried in the ground. Slowly the original material (usually calcium phosphate) is replaced by other minerals (such as silica) carried by water seeping slowly down through the earth.

Interestingly, different minerals can produce quite startlingly different effects. For example, all the dinosaur bones dug from the patch of rock known as the Morrison Formation in Wyoming, USA, are shiny and black. Other fossils may be dark or light brown or green; or they may even have been turned multicoloured by the presence of iron pyrites.

So that's the basic principle. But how do the bones get into that position in the first place? Here's how a number of different forms of fossilization take place.

Sedimentation

When a creature dies, it usually decays or gets eaten by other creatures very quickly. If this doesn't happen, sedimentation may occur. The creature is very quickly covered by mud or other sediments; this usually happens in locations such as the mouth of a river, the bottom of a muddy lake or swamp, or on the sea floor, where the debris of plankton and thousands of dead bodies forms its own mud.

Here's how sedimentation produces fossils:

(1) Our creature dies and its body sinks to the sea floor. If it doesn't just break up in the current or get eaten, it may become covered by mud and other debris, and this stops any further decay by keeping oxygen out.

(2) The lower layers of sediment, pressed down under the weight of the bodies above, very slowly turn to rock. (Sometimes, of course, this weight just crushes our potential fossil – we told you that fossilization was a tricky business.) The creature's bones dissolve and leave a hollow mould which may be filled by minerals as they trickle down through the new rock, forming a solid, natural cast. Above, more and more sedimentation takes place over and over again, creating more and more layers of sedimentary rock. This may very well take hundreds of thousands of years.

(3) Under the influence of pressure from the likes of Continental Drift (see page 54), volcanoes or earthquakes, the sea retreats and the land is raised or lowered, folded or buckled. Safe within its layer of rock, our fossil is carried along with this process. This may take millions of years.

(4) The rock layer containing our fossil gets exposed to the outside air. This may be caused by various means: covering layers may be worn away, to reveal the bone-filled layer beneath, perhaps by wind erosion; or perhaps a fold or a fault – where softer rock is worn away by the wind or a river, for example – may reveal the many layers present. If the rock forms part of a cliff or escarpment, our fossil may even simply fall out and lie around in the open, just waiting for an eager young dinosaur investigator to come along and scoop it up for their collection.

Other types of fossilization

The vast majority of fossils are made by the good old sedimentation process. However, there are also a number of other methods. In many of these other cases, the processes of decay are only paused, rather than stopped; when such fossils are exposed to the air again, the process of decay soon causes them to crumble! As you can perhaps imagine, this can cause palaeontologists to feel very unhappy.

Amber: This is the fossilized resin or sap from an ancient plant or tree. The earliest fossil ambers occurred in the early Cretaceous Period and they are now sometimes found, buried in the ground or just washed up on the seashore among the pebbles. As you'll know if you were paying attention at the start of *Jurassic Park* (rather than just scoffing popcorn and waiting for the first computer-generated dinosaurs to turn up), creatures that were caught in the sap as it flowed down the tree have been found, still imprisoned within their orange, glassy tomb, millions of years later. Unlike what happens in the film, no one has ever found a mosquito full of dinosaur blood – at least not yet – but fossils which have been found inside amber have included feathers, plants, insects, spiders and even small lizards and frogs. These days, amber is also carved and shaped for the jewellery trade, and large lumps of it can be worth a lot of money.

Coal and oil: Known as a fossil fuel, coal is the fossilized result of trees being slowly crushed and compressed over millions of years while their wood is replaced by minerals. This was the fate of plants which died in freshwater swamps, back at the dawn of time. In the thick, muddy water the absence of oxygen prevented their decaying, so they formed thick, black peat instead. Some peat bogs were then buried under sedimentary rock, which crushed the peat and turned it into coal. Coal may not be very exciting, of course, but contained within it there may be an incredible variety of small fossils, from other plants to spiders, insects and even fish, all dating from the Carboniferous Period (see the section on page 56 for details of the different ages of the Earth). Coal miners often find these fossils in the course of their work.

Oil, another fossil fuel, is formed in a similar way, except that, instead of plants, the important layer is one of tiny fossil plankton, whose crushed bodies are transformed into oil-rich *kerogen*. Yes, that's right, the oil that cars run on and everything plastic in your house is made from the bodies of fossils. Weird!

Ice: In the deep-frozen wastes of northern Siberia the ground is permanently frozen (permafrost). Below the surface of such a harsh and frigid land, scientists have found the bodies of mammoths, perfectly preserved despite the creatures becoming extinct some 12,000 years ago, and in recent years Russian scientists have even uncovered clumps of reddish-brown mammoth hair. The ice-fields of Antarctica and Greenland have also yielded frozen remains. There are few frozen fossils from more distant times than that of the mammoths, however; the Earth has enjoyed several very warm periods which may have caused previously frozen spots to thaw out, allowing the normal processes of decay to destroy older fossils.

Mummification: In a few rare cases, very dry conditions have been known to preserve creatures for several thousand years. The best places for mummification tend to be distant caves or the depths of cold deserts such as the Gobi or the Atacama. Mummification rarely preserves fossils for very long and, once exposed to more normal conditions, the fossils quickly decay to nothing. However, unlike other processes, mummification can prove very effective at preserving even the softest parts of an animal. For example, in the British Museum in London there is the grisly mummified foot of an ancient moa from an isolated cave in New Zealand, complete with horrible hairy skin still attached! (It's enough to put you off your Sunday lunch for ever!)

Petrification: Also known as 'silicification', this is basically what happens when an organism, particularly a tree or a plant, is turned to stone. This does not happen through some legendary magical transformation – some snake-haired old woman going around giving things the evil eye, for example – but through a process similar to the fossilization of sedimentary rock. What usually takes place is that a fallen tree-trunk gets covered in volcanic ash or silt which then seeps inside the wood, slowly replacing the vegetable matter with silica. Petrification tends not to produce anything but very crude fossils, with few details preserved.

Tar: Similar to crude oil, this sticky black gunk is sometimes found on the surface in the form of a pool. At the famous La Brea tar-pits in modern-day

Los Angeles in the USA, hundreds of creatures were caught in the tar about 20,000 years ago. Their bodies were preserved in the lower layers as they solidified over the millennia, leaving them perfectly preserved for us to dig up.

Fossil-bearing Rocks

Logically speaking, if you wanted to find fossils and didn't quite know where to start looking, all you would need to do would be to work out which types of rock usually hold fossils, look up where they are on a geological map, then go and dig them up. So, bearing this in mind, which rocks are the best at preserving fossils?

If you took a slice down through the Earth, from the surface to close to its molten core, it would look much like a slice of Neapolitan ice-cream – but far less tasty. There would be layer upon layer of various types of rock laid out in stripes. Rock is formed by the accumulation of minerals, such as quartzes or feldspars, which are made up of many common elements such as oxygen, carbon, iron, silicon and sodium. There are three general classes of rock, and each class comes in a number of varieties. At any one place on the Earth all three classes of rock may be represented, having slowly formed and covered one another over millions of years.

The three main classes of rock are as follows. (The one that's of most interest to a dinosaur investigator should immediately be apparent!)

Igneous Rocks: These are formed from molten lava, after it solidifies, either on or beneath the Earth's surface. The extremely hard rock, granite, formed at great depths where immense pressure squeezes it together and makes it very dense, is a typical igneous rock.

Sedimentary Rocks: Such rocks are formed when layers of sand, mud or organic material (including the bones of creatures) settle on to a surface after being eroded by wind or water. Limestone, mudstone and sandstone are typical examples.

Metamorphic Rocks: This class of rock is formed from one of the other two types. They are sedimentary or igneous rocks that have been modified either by extreme heat or by crushing pressure, generated by movements in the Earth's crust.

Find the right rocks . . .

As you will undoubtedly have guessed, most fossils are found in sedimentary rocks. However, tracking down such rocks and fossils is not simple.

Most rocks of this sort were deposited in ocean basins; so these rock formations preserve only those few dinosaur bodies which were swept out to sea. It's far more likely that most sedimentary rocks will contain the fossils of nothing more exciting than sea creatures and plants (not that this is such a bad thing, really; it's just that, well, although fossils are great, it's the big dinosaurs that we're really after). A sedimentary rock like chalk, for example, is made up of little more than the bones of uncountable numbers of tiny sea creatures like plankton and shrimps which died and fell to the sea floor over tens of millions of years. Within rock like chalk, however, there may be larger lumps which retain their shape. These are often 'nodules', where rock has formed round a larger fossil, such as a shell or a bone.

If you want to find dinosaurs, you will have to find an area of sedimentary rock that was formed by deposits of mud and silt laid down by a river or stream, in an area subject to constant flooding or covered by wind-blown sand or volcanic ash, or at the bottom of a stagnant lake or pond.

Oh, and of course you will then have to find rocks in formations that are exposed on the surface, whether through a fold in the crust or in a layer exposed by a cliff face. Many prime fossil-bearing rocks are covered with forests or the oceans or are buried deep under younger rocks. During mining operations or at very large construction sites, fossils are sometimes found many hundreds of metres underground. Indeed, most of the major dinosaur discoveries in heavily developed countries like Britain are made in this way these days.

That brings us to a final point. If you want to find a dinosaur, the theory goes, find a site where a big lump of sedimentary rock has been exposed on the Earth's surface. In many parts of the Western world, those that have been surveyed and mapped by geo-logists, this is easy to say. The trouble is, these are likely to be the first places where previous dinosaur investigators have looked. If there were any truly major discoveries to be made, they have already been done.

However, don't lose heart. There are many millions of smaller fossils waiting out there for you to find – and who knows what else may be hidden away in those tantalizing layers of sedimentary rock?

... And you might find some fossils

You'll find fossils in most places where sedimentary rocks are exposed on the surface. Sedimentary rocks include many different types of limestone, sandstone, clays and shales. Such rocks are probably more common than you suppose. Much of the southern part of Britain, for example, is comprised of such rocks, and in fact there are patches of sedimentary rock all over the country.

The very best places to look for fossils are those where the underlying strata have been exposed only recently, or out-of-the-way places where few other fossil-hunters have dared to venture. In a small country like Britain this may prove a challenge, but there will always be unexpectedly good sites for your searches.

Close to water: Wave-washed cliffs and shoreline rocks are great places to search for fossils, because the sea may be constantly exposing fresh parts of the rock. Just be extremely careful that you don't get swept out to sea by the tide or brained by a chalky rock-slide, will you?

Less commonly, rivers may expose new fossils as they cut into the bank – though retrieving such fossils may prove very tricky. As an extreme example, consider the incredible Grand Canyon in the USA, where several million years of layers have been exposed by the deep gouges made, kilometres down into the rock, by the Colorado river.

Deserts: Out in the driest parts of the world the wind can wear away great areas of cold- or heat-cracked rock surfaces. The pace of erosion may be extremely slow (it may take centuries for the weather to remove even the thinnest layer of rock), but it can take place over very large areas at the same time. The major problem with exploring such areas is that almost always they are very far from civilization and require a long-distance journey to visit.

Rocky landscapes: These may be closer at hand – national parks and areas of outstanding natural beauty are often reachable on a day trip, even if you live in an inner city. However, some areas may have laws banning the removal of fossils, to stop areas becoming damaged (remember, you swore to uphold the Golden Rules on page 10).

Man-made sites: Quarries and mines are very good sources of fossils, and many famous discoveries have been made in sites like these. For the amateur fossil-hunter, permission to dig may prove troublesome to obtain. There aren't all that many Saturday jobs going, down the mines any more, even for keen dinosaur investigator types.

A long way away: The very best places to look for dinosaur fossils are where other investigators have not been. Consequently, the search for the very best fossils takes dedicated palaeontologists to the furthest and most distant parts of the planet. For example, many of the major finds this century have been made in the outlying fringes of the far Gobi Desert in Mongolia. Mounting expeditions to such places can be both expensive and time-consuming. It may require a journey by plane, train or truck, lasting many days. And of course there's no real guarantee that you'll actually find anything when you get there! These days, even with the help of satellite photographs and extremely detailed geological maps, it is common for teams of palaeontologists to send out a couple of experts first in order to have a scout around and assess the potential of an area.

The strangest places: Many fossils are revealed by the strange twists and folds in the Earth's crust. This can produce very strange effects. Dinosaur tracks, for example, have been found going straight up vertical cliffs – where the rock has been folded in this way, it is now vertical rather than horizontal. With the changing of the continents (see the next page), fossils can turn up in locations which are now very different from the way they were 65 million or more years ago. It has long been recorded that seashells and other fossils have been found at the tops of mountains; the bones of fish have been found in the depths of the Sahara and other deserts!

In Colorado in the United States Mine, in 1937, some extremely fascinating dinosaur tracks were found. There was just one teensy problem: they were above everyone's head, poking out of the ceiling! As you may perhaps imagine, digging them out proved highly problematical.

A World of Fossils

If they had anything in common with their reptilian descendants, it is that dinosaurs lived just about everywhere, on land-masses across the whole planet. Geological evidence indeed confirms that their favourite habitats were plains, forests, beaches, swamps and deserts. Furthermore, let's not forget all those sea-dwelling reptiles like Ichthyosaurs.

However, 65 million or more years ago the positions of the continents were very different from what they are today (see page 54). We can't just think, simply because one type of dinosaur liked living in a big swamp in a cool climate, that if we start digging around somewhere like the mouth of the River Danube we'll find hundreds of dinosaurs. The face of the world has changed time and again since the dinosaurs were around. Back in their day, the world was far more temperate. There may not have been any ice at either of the poles; it's no wonder we find fossils in Antarctica and in the Canadian Arctic. Great, warm, inland seas covered much of the land.

No, if we want to find dinosaurs and other fossils, we need to pin-point the places where rocks of an age similar to that of the dinosaurs are found today.

Places to look in Britain

So come on, you're undoubtedly shouting out loud, where exactly *are* the best places to look? Well, check out the four simplified geological maps we've included on pages 46 and 47. They will tell you which types of rock are where. Obviously, if you are serious about tracking down dinosaurs or other important fossils, you will need far more detailed geological maps, rather like Ordnance Survey maps, which show every last detail of the make-up of the underlying rock. Your local library or geological society may be able to help with these.

If you just want to find a few common-or-garden fossils, however, there are many places where you can look. Traditionally, the best areas for finding fossils (and the occasional dinosaur as well) are the early Cretaceous shales and chalks that run along the south coast, and especially around Kimmeridge Bay and Lyme Regis in Dorset, and on the southern side of the Isle of Wight. As one example, the widely reported discovery in May 1997 of a massive selection of Diplodocus footprints was made at a quarry near Corfe Castle in Dorset.

As a more general rule, all around the British coastline, wherever there are cliffs to expose the lower layers of sedimentary rock, investigators have found a wide variety of fossils, from tiny sea-urchins to bones and teeth from marine animals and reptiles. Maybe that trip to the seaside with your Gran for the school holidays doesn't sound like such a dull option after all, eh?

Older fossils have been found in other locations. The oldest sedimentary rocks in Britain are in Wales; indeed, that area's rocks have given their name to several geological periods (see later). Welsh rocks seem to be especially crammed with fossil trilobites and molluscs.

Although those are the most famous places for finding fossils in the UK, in fact much of the country is made up of rock which can – in theory, at least – contain fossils from the various eras of the Earth's history. Have a look at these maps and see whether your house is standing on something. Just one word of warning: don't just start digging in your cellar – chances are that the right rocks are to be found many hundreds of metres underneath your house, and your folks will *not* be pleased!

Here are the maps. We'll explain which rocks from the various periods may hold which types of fossil in just a moment.

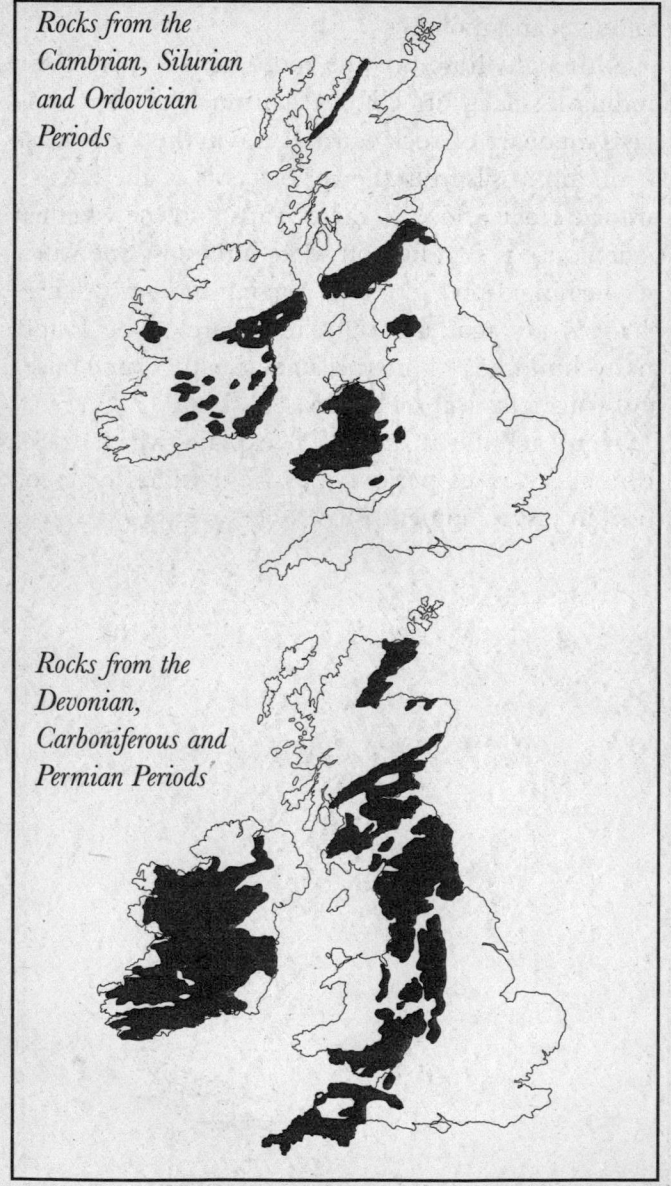

Rocks from the Cambrian, Silurian and Ordovician Periods

Rocks from the Devonian, Carboniferous and Permian Periods

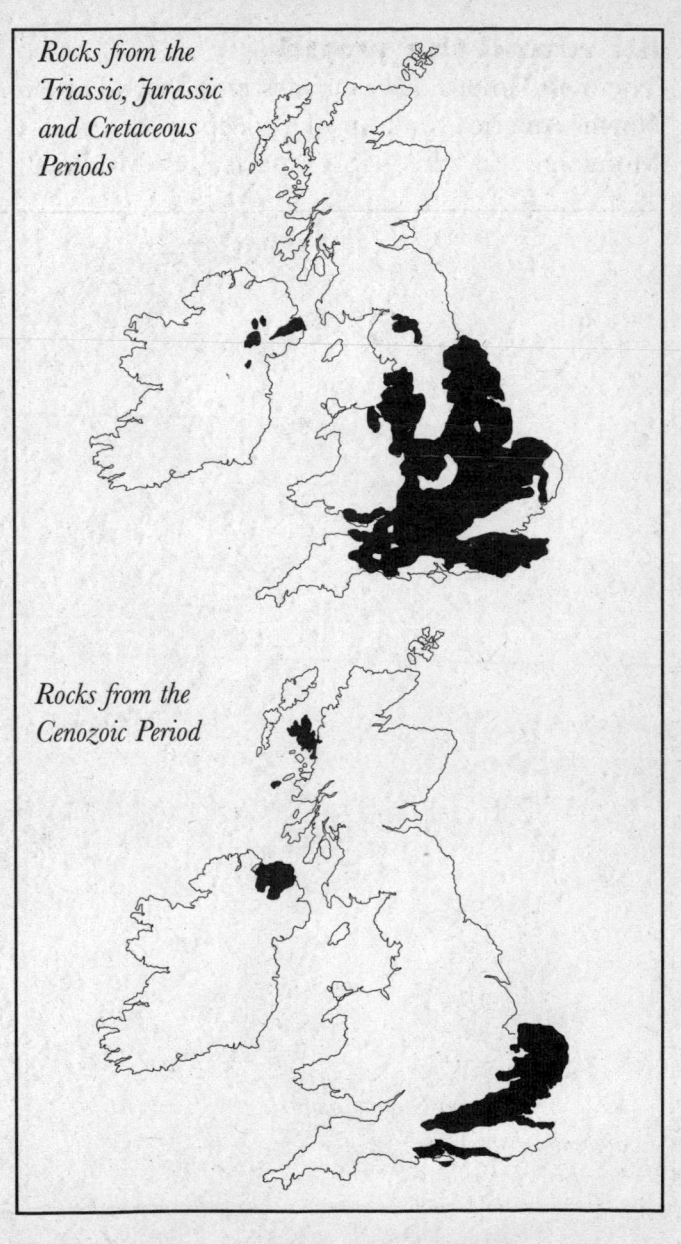

Rocks from the Triassic, Jurassic and Cretaceous Periods

Rocks from the Cenozoic Period

All round the world

The most famous dinosaur sites in the world are in North America and in the deepest deserts of Mongolia. In the USA, parts of Montana,

Sites of the most important dinosaur discoveries

Wyoming and Utah have been declared special National Monuments, and holidays are offered to would-be dinosaur investigators who wish to pop along and have a go at digging out some bones – at

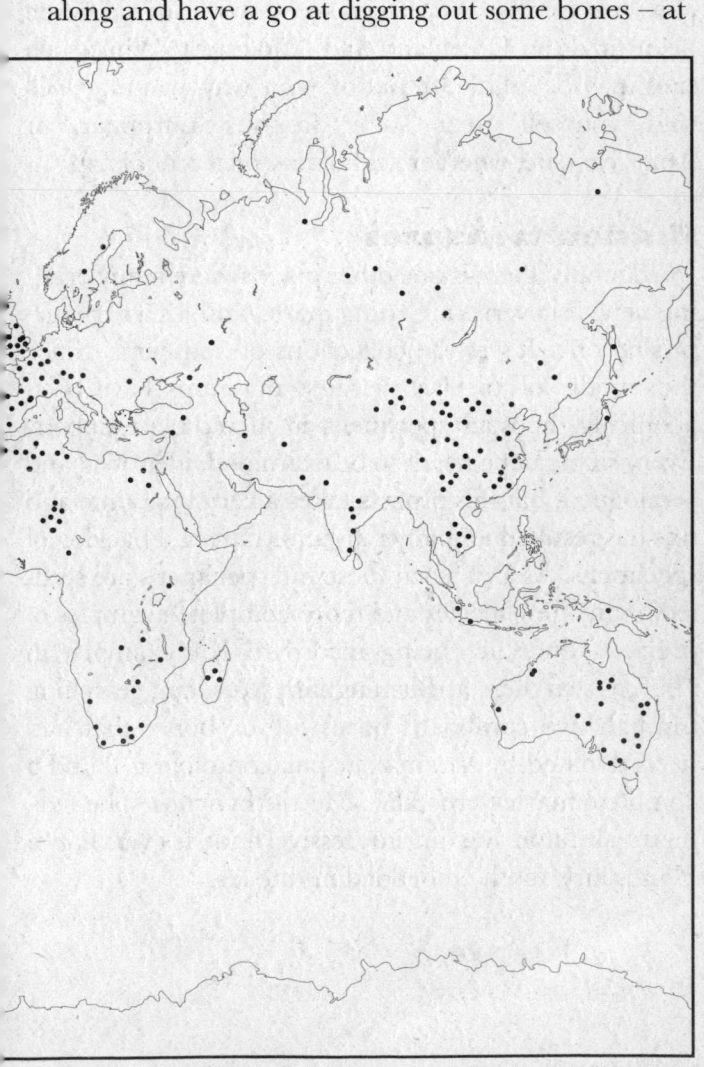

a healthy price, of course.

However, dinosaurs have now been found pretty much all over the world, as the map on the previous page makes clear. As you can see, discoveries have even been made in Greenland and Antarctica! While such sites may be a little bit out of your way, you may well find yourself near some famous European or American site, whether on holiday or a school trip.

Hidden treasures

Incidentally, there is one other place where many exciting new discoveries are being made, and it's a very surprising one. It's in the collections of museums! Since the middle of the last century, museums have been acquiring dinosaur specimens in incredible numbers. Every single bone needs to be examined, identified and catalogued, but this process takes a very long time and this has resulted in many museums having a backlog of specimens. As and when these old specimens are studied, many new species and more complete examples of previous finds are being recorded! For example, in 1997, researchers at Birmingham Museum, searching through two cardboard boxes full of bones that had been donated by an amateur palaeontologist, found a complete marine crocodile, Metriorhynchus. The five-metre skeleton was an impressive find: it even had a Plesiosaur's tooth embedded in one leg.

Land of the Dinosaurs

So that's where the fossils of dinosaurs and other creatures may well be found nowadays (in theory, at least).

But have you ever wondered how it is that creatures of the same sort can be found both in deepest Asia and in North America? How the bones of a Stegosaurus can be found embedded in limestone in Germany, while footprints from a Stegosaurus can turn up on a plain in Australia?

That's a thorny problem which had been bothering scientists and naturalists for centuries. Eventually, however, a German scientist called Alfred Wegener came up with a theory which, although not quite 100 per cent proven, seems to explain very well what happened. And it's a very startling one.

Do a little experiment for us, would you. Stand up, and then stand very still for a minute. Feel that? No? Huh! Some investigator you are. What you should have felt was the distinct sensation of movement – because even though you were standing still, the ground you are standing on is moving!

OK, that wasn't a serious experiment (we hope your own researches are far less silly). The rate of movement is very small. But the continents are indeed moving across the surface of the planet. This is 'Continental Drift'.

Have you ever looked at the outline of Africa and wondered why its western coastline seems roughly to match up with the eastern coast of South America? Go ahead, take a look at the world map on pages 48–49. See? Spooky – yet it's not a coincidence. Millions of years ago, those two great continents were indeed joined together!

Scientists looking into Wegener's theory found that there are very similar rocks in Africa and South America – so similar, in fact, that they could have been part of the same ancient mountain range. More obscurely, magnetic forces within the rocks of those mountains all point in the same direction. Add to that all the many examples of the same species being found in very distant parts of the world, and the theory of Continental Drift seems to hold true.

But how does it all move? Well, surprising as it may seem, the Earth's crust isn't a single, solid, thick layer. It comes in pieces, like sections of a huge irregular jigsaw puzzle. These pieces or 'plates' are all wearing way at each other. Where they rub together, earthquakes are caused. Where they push together, they form mountains where previously there were none. Where the plates pull apart, there may be trenches or they may allow lava to come to the surface to form volcanoes. Satellite maps of the ocean floor reveal great ridges in the Atlantic and deep trenches in the Pacific, formed as the continents pull apart.

Now, as our silly experiment above revealed, the plates are not moving especially fast. The Atlantic is widening between North America and Europe by about two centimetres a year, for example. However, multiply that by millions of years and you'll realize that the world the dinosaurs knew looked very different indeed!

Way back in the Permian, as our maps on pages 54 and 55 show, the world's land-masses were a single huge super-continent; the scientists call it Pangaea. Slowly this was pulled apart, forming, first, two large continents (Gondwanaland and Laurasia), then many more, until slowly but surely the world as we know it today was formed.

What's more, as time continues (though we will not be around to see it happen) the continents will continue to move. In a further 65 million years' time, the Earth's land-masses will look very different again.

CONTINENTAL DRIFT

As you can see, the continents move and change continually. Any predictions for how our world will look 65 or 180 million years from now?

180 million years ago

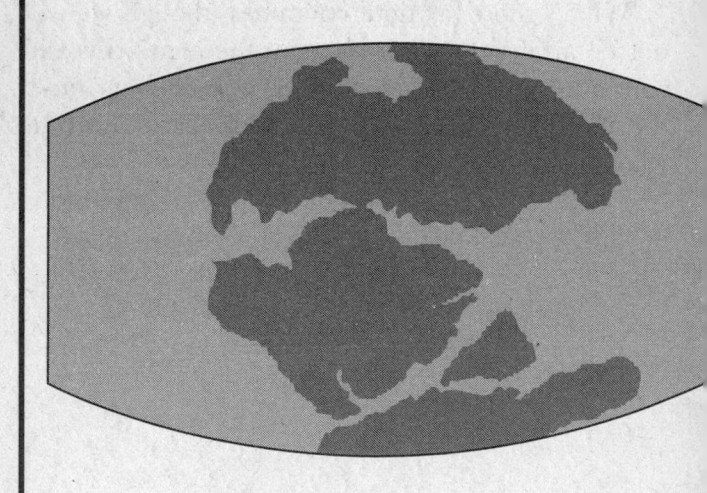

million years ago

oday

A Brief History of Time

Since we're going on about time at present, we should really explain a little more about how geologists see it, and explain the history of planet Earth in a little more detail.

Time is measured in Millions of Years Ago (or mya for short). If you think that's a long time ago, you'd be right, but the measurements go back even further: all the way back to the first development of life on this planet. It may strike you that this is 'relative time' – that is, you're measuring back from wherever you are currently standing, so in one million years' time all your measurements will be out by one million. But now we'll stop thinking about that, as it's making our brains ache. That's the problem with this time stuff: it does make great demands on the bonce.

Anyway, as far as scientists are able currently to estimate, the planet Earth was formed about 4,600 mya. For a long time nothing happened, just a whole bunch of chemicals slowing and cooling to form the different elements, which then clustered together to form rocks. Life has been present on Earth for at least 3,000 million years – though it must be said that, for the first 2,000 million years, there was nothing more complex knocking about than microscopic bacteria.

Eras and periods

Scientists have managed to work all this out from the age of different rocks. This is done by using various calculations based on the decay of radioactivity in different elements and other extremely clever stuff we won't go into here. As new methods of measurement are being perfected, some estimates get gently corrected, but the figures are accurate for now.

On the next page you will find a more detailed breakdown of the different sections of time, from the creation of this planet right up to the present day. You'll see it is (mainly) divided into periods and eras.

A *period* is the time it took for a particular type of rock to be laid down. Since rocks form very slowly indeed, each of these periods lasts for tens of millions of years. Most periods are named after the place where their rocks were first studied. So, the Devonian is named after the county of Devon in England; the Cambrian after the Roman name for Wales; the Jurassic after the Jura Mountains in Switzerland.

These periods are grouped together into *eras*, which are named after the kind of life that was present at the time. They are as follows: the *Azoic* (which means 'without life'), the *Archaeozoic* ('ancient life'), the *Proterozoic* ('former life'), the *Palaeozoic* ('early life'), the *Mesozoic* ('middle life') and the *Cenozoic* ('recent life').

Periods themselves are then broken down into individual *epochs*. The very last epoch of recorded time is the Holocene, which is still going on. It's the period we live in, and it started only 10,000 years ago, when mankind first began to show signs of civilization in the form of agriculture and settlement dwelling. We'll be living in the Holocene for a little while yet.

Timeline of Earth history

MYA	Era	Period	Developments
4,600	Azoic		Earth cools, rocks solidify, no life
2,300	Archaeozoic		Bacteria
1,400	Proterozoic		Algae, first plants
570	Palaeozoic	Cambrian	Molluscs, jellyfish, trilobites
510		Ordovician	Coral, first jawless fish, starfish, ammonites
440		Silurian	Plants on land, insects on land, snails
408		Devonian	Fish dominant, ferns, first amphibians
362		Carboniferous**	Amphibians dominant, first flying insects
290		Permian	First reptiles, conifers
248	Mesozoic	Triassic	First true mammals, first dinosaurs and pterosaurs
213		Jurassic	Giant dinosaurs

143		Cretaceous	Dinosaurs dominant, first birds, first flowering plants, first modern insects
65	Cenozoic	Palaeocene*	Dinosaurs and many others extinct; mammals diversify
57		Eocene*	Whales, first true primates
35		Oligocene*	
23		Miocene*	
5		Pliocene*	First human ancestors
2		Pleistocene*	Java man, Neanderthal man, modern man
0.01		Holocene*	Development of human agriculture

* Because they are so short, the divisions of the Cenozoic are termed epochs rather than periods; up until the Pliocene is the Tertiary Period; since then it's been the Quaternary Period.

** Sometimes split into the Mississippian and Pennsylvanian Periods for no real reason other than to be confusing.

You Want to Call It *What*?

The study of fossils is a science, so it is governed by a number of procedures to ensure that no one gets confused and no information is muddled up or lost. One of the most important of these procedures is in the naming of fossils.

Many creatures have been given common, every-day names, whether they be a tabby cat, a grizzly bear or a golden eagle. However, in different languages these names will come out differently, which may cause yet more confusion.

So there's a better system, and it's one that scientists use. Every single creature known to science on this planet has a specific, two-part, Latin name. No other creature has that name, which is the same in every language in the world (or, at least, it's in another, very specific language). What's more, looking at that name, you can immediately see which creatures are related to it. Not surprisingly, fossil creatures, including dinosaurs, have also had these names bestowed upon them.

These names always come in two parts. First, there's the *genus* (marked by a capital letter): that's the greater family which the creature belongs to. Secondly, there's the *species* (never spelt with a capital letter): that's the particular type (of whatever animal) it is. So, for example and in English translation, the genus might be a Bear, whereas the species might indicate it is indeed a grizzly. You may well already be familiar with dinosaurs such as Triceratops,

Apatosaurus, Tyrannosaurus, and so on. These names are the genus; within the Triceratops family, for example, there are a number of different but related dinosaurs, including *Triceratops alticornis*, *Triceratops prorsus* and *Triceratops horridus* (obviously the ugly one of the family).

These days, all new dinosaur names are governed by the International Code of Zoological Nomenclature (ICZN), which ensures that no two creatures have the same name. In general, the first person to describe a new type is allowed to name it. Such a name may be derived from the person who found it, the place where it was found, or a description in Greek or Latin of what the creature looked like.

The case of the vanishing Brontosaurus

Before all that business about allowing the first person to describe a creature to give it its proper name came in, there were a few confusions, and none more so than in the case of the Brontosaurus.

To put it bluntly, there is no such dinosaur as the Brontosaurus. Yes, yes, calm down, we all know there is, and what it looks like. The trouble is, that's not its proper name. In 1877, Othniel Marsh described a new four-footed dinosaur, based on certain fragments, which he called 'Apatosaurus ajax'. Two years later he found another set of fragments, from a new creature, which he called 'Brontosaurus excelsius' (or 'thunder reptile'). This was a better example, and sketches and models of it were made.

The public took a shine to the enormous new creatures, and the name Brontosaurus became very widely known.

In 1899, soon after Marsh died, one of his colleagues, Samuel Williston, realized that both creatures were of the same genus! Marsh simply hadn't spotted the similarity. And, because scientists play by the rules and since Apatosaurus was the first name given, that's what Brontosaurus became. So now Brontosaurus doesn't exist any more. Ah!

Goodbye Brontosaurus, hello Apatosaurus!

Know your dinosaur

As they are often derived from Latin, many dinosaur names have specific translations and mean something quite unusual. Here's what many of the most famous dinosaurs' names mean . . .

Allosaurus	strange reptile
Ankylosaurus	fused reptile
Apatosaurus	deceptive reptile
Archaeopteryx	ancient wing
Baryonyx	heavy claw
Brachiosaurus	arm reptile
Compsognathus	pretty jaw
Deinonychus	terrible claw
Dimetrodon	two long teeth
Diplodocus	double beam
Dromaeosaurus	running reptile
Gallimimus	chicken-mimic
Hesperornis	western bird
Iguanodon	iguana tooth
Maiasaurus	mother reptile
Megalosaurus	giant reptile
Oviraptor	egg stealer
Pachycephalosaurus	thick-head reptile
Plateosaurus	flat reptile
Plesiosaurus	ribbon reptile
Polacanthus	many spines
Protoceratops	first horned
Pterodactyl	wing finger
Seismosaurus	earthquake reptile

Stegosaurus.................................roofed reptile

Torosaurus...................................bull reptile

Triceratops.................................three-horned face

Tyrannosaurus............................tyrant reptile

Velociraptor...............................speedy predator

Spot the Fossil

In the next few pages, we're going to look at the various types of fossils that exist, if only we could find them. We've divided each section into the specific types; coincidentally, this breaks down pretty much into the order in which such creatures first appeared (see the Time Chart, back on page 58).

The very earliest life on Earth, so scientists theorize, was formed when, amidst the chemical soup of the oceans, chemical reactions became so complicated that they formed a living creature. It might well have had a single cell.

However, fossils of such creatures, where they survive at all, are really of interest only to scientists looking at the very earliest periods of Earth's development. There is little that is fascinating about microscopic blobs of rock to the amateur dinosaur investigator!

FOSSIL PLANTS

Although almost certainly life existed before them, the oldest definite fossils are of blue-green algae, from 2,700 million years ago. Found in graphite limestone beneath farmland, near Bulawayo in Zimbabwe, this stuff is just a collection of thousands of tiny, one-celled organisms. You know that green scum which collects in fish tanks? That's algae. Not entirely thrilling, we think you'll agree.

Different and ever more complicated forms of algae developed over the years, and they are to be found in rocks from every era and period of Earth's history. Some algae are important age-indicators in rocks and are used extensively in the oil industry in the search for more new oilfields.

Fossil algae

Fossil remains are generally dull (not least because they're often too small to see!) but a few types may be found, clustered together to produce attractive regular formations. A fossil of Mastopora, for example, looks like a dome made up of irregular dents, rather like a large stone golf ball. Acanthochonia is even prettier, consisting of a sphere of diamond-shaped facets arranged in a spiral. Both are found in Silurian rocks.

Eventually the algae became more and more complicated, and they developed into primitive plants. From floating green scum to seaweed, all vegetation lived in or on the sea; slowly, however, plants learnt to breathe air and they moved up on to the land as well – a long time before other living creatures like fish slithered up on to the beaches.

Before the Jurassic Period, the landscape was littered with nothing but green plants and trees. Among the dominant plants at the time of the dinosaurs were the horsetail (this grew up to 18 metres tall, far loftier than its more usual modern height of 1.5 metres), the monkey-puzzle tree, ferns, club-mosses and lycopods (a few species of which grew to a height of 40 metres!).

Flowers and fruits were late developers, not

appearing until the middle of the Jurassic Period. Furthermore, since they were very soft items, it is very rare to find them preserved as a fossil, or even as a vague imprint.

Fossil plants

The best place to find fossil vegetation is in coal. If picked out against a darker or lighter background, a fossil leaf or branch can look very pretty indeed.

Conifers: The earliest examples come from the Carboniferous, but pine cones and other seed-carriers have been found from all eras.

Ferns: The oldest ferns are from the Devonian Period, but more than 10,000 species are still around these days, all of them in forms that are very similar to way back then. In Carboniferous times, however, some species grew to the same height as modern trees. Fern fossils are very common.

Flowers: Because they are so delicate, and they also appeared much later than other types of plant, fossil flowers are far rarer than fossil leaves and stalks.

Leaves: Many examples from tens of millions of years ago look just like modern leaves. Again, they are common, but many fossil leaves can be very pretty.

Seeds: Fossil plant seeds are quite common; since they look like lumpy little pebbles, however, they aren't always the most interesting fossils to collect.

THE FIRST INVERTEBRATES

In rocks from the Cambrian Period, simple creatures had developed. First there were amoebas and plankton, tiny, wriggly, worm-like blobs. After another 50 million years or so, however, these had developed into slightly more complicated forms. Slowly but surely a whole range of invertebrates (this means 'creatures without proper backbones') developed and spread throughout the waters of the world.

Invertebrate fossils

Brachiopods: Around 250 types of these sea-bed-dwelling creatures are known to modern science – but over 30,000 fossil types! Typically, they have shell-like bodies which are attached to the sea floor. It's no wonder that so many were buried and preserved for posterity. Other brachiopods include living sponges, the creatures from which we get our bath-time loofahs!

Corals: Since primordial times, corals have formed massive but incredibly intricate communities on the sea floor, clustering together. The oldest corals are from the Ordovician Period; these days they turn up as patterns within some types of limestone.

Related creatures like sea anemones and jellyfish are thought to have developed around the same time but, since they lack hard skeletons, they have never been preserved. Fossil coral is found throughout the planet – remember, the sea has covered every part of the land at one time or another.

Molluscs: A very diverse group, nearly all have shells enclosing a soft body. Usually the soft inside is lost during fossilization, leaving only the actual shell. This type of creature may be a gastropod or a bivalve – snails and shellfish, basically. Molluscs first emerged at the beginning of the Cambrian Period, about 550 million years ago. Typical fossils include oysters and whelks, cowries and conches, and snails from both the sea and the land. They are extremely common by the seaside, in chalk and so on.

Cephalopods: As molluscs developed, one branch evolved into the cephalopods, sea-crossing relatives of the modern octopus, squid and cuttlefish. Among the most successful were relatives of the modern nautilus, the ammonites. These coiled-shell creatures teemed around the oceans from the Devonian to the Cretaceous. The largest grew to over 2 metres in diameter, which is pretty big for an overgrown underwater snail!

Ammonites are particularly well represented in the fossil record. Little is known about their soft parts, but their coiled shells are very common indeed – which is handy, because they can be very beautiful. Many fossil ammonites have been found with their shells replaced by shiny iron pyrites, which gives them a multicoloured look. The last ammonites became extinct, very suddenly and for unknown

Five different types of ammonite from the Cretaceous Period

reasons, at the end of the Cretaceous Period, just as the dinosaurs did.

Echinoderms: That name describes a distinctive group of sea-creatures, including starfish and brittle-stars, sea-urchins and sea-cucumbers. Unlike the rest of the animal kingdom, almost all of them have a five-pointed symmetry – think of a starfish's five arms, for example. Many have hard exoskeletons, called 'tests' (no, don't panic, nothing to do with exams) so they are preserved for modern times. Among other types, crinoids or sea-lilies were once very common, as the fossil record proves. They were like living plants and looked like a long-armed starfish stuck on the end of a long stem, which was often attached to a rock or driftwood. These days, most sea-lilies have lost the long stem and crawl about as featherstars. Fossil sea-urchins are very common along the seashore.

FOSSIL ARTHROPODS

As the invertebrates evolved, their bodies became more complex. Eventually one distinct group, the arthropods, developed into many of the most successful invertebrate types known today to science. These include insects, spiders, crabs, scorpions, lobsters, millipedes, barnacles, lice and others. The arthropods are an extremely varied group, but only those types which included exoskeletons – such as trilobites, and crustaceans like crabs and lobsters – have been preserved, except in rare cases. The first fossil arthropods appear in Ordovician rock, which is named, rather obscurely, after the Ordovices, a historical Celtic tribe who once lived in that part of Wales where such rock was first identified.

Arthropod fossils

Crustaceans: Fossil crabs and barnacles are very common; later, from the Jurassic Period, fossil shrimps and lobsters have also been found. All these creatures look very similar to their modern counterparts.

Trilobites: These odd creatures, looking a little like flattened shrimps or woodlice with their ribbed, shelled bodies, get their name because their hard exoskeletons appear to be divided into three distinct parts (three lobes, geddit?). As they grew older, trilobites increased in size by adding another segment to their body; some fossils have been found up to 1 metre long, though others have been found barely 2 millimetres in size. Fossil trilobites are found in rocks from the Cambrian to the Permian. During that time they seem to have been very successful; scientists now wonder whether their eyes, which seem to be highly developed, might have given them an advantage, even in the murky seas. Whatever, there are certainly a lot of fossil trilobites about; they make up about half of all fossils from the Cambrian Period from all over the globe.

Insects: Although they now teem over the face of the Earth, insects were actually very late starters and did not move on to the land until late in the Devonian Period. Because of their small size and soft parts, not all that many fossil insects are found. However, there are a few of note: fossil cockroaches are found quite often, and they look much like their modern counterparts. More beautiful are primitive fossilized dragonflies, including a few rare finds of the massive Meganeura, whose wings were up to 73 centimetres across!

Chelicerates: This family includes the spiders and scorpions; they started as sea-scorpions, then moved on to the land. It's possible that the first creatures to ever walk on land, in fact, were some predatory sea-scorpions. Because of their softer bodies, they are far less common as fossils, though their impressions are sometimes to be found in rocks from coal seams and, very occasionally, encased in amber.

FISH WITH EVERYTHING

When fish came along, around 500 million years ago, the whole course of evolution took a giant leap forward. It's possible they developed from shell-less echinoderms which evolved with some of their bones inside their body – the first creatures with backbones (or vertebrates, as scientists call them). The very first fish were similar to modern species in many ways: they had gills to allow them to breathe water, and they swam using primitive fins. However, the early fish were covered in bony armour, and they did not have solid jaws.

In the Silurian (named after another ancient Welsh tribe, the Silures), the first true fish appeared. The placoderms had proper, evenly paired fins and proper toothed jaws; however, they still had bony plates round their heads, and they looked rather like heavily armoured catfish.

The Devonian Period is known as the Age of Fishes, however, for the sheer variety of species which teemed in the ocean. While a few gathered around the coastline and tried, for some unfathomable reason, to flop out of the water, in the depths all manner of new types of fish were evolving, including most that we can still reel in today.

Typical fish fossils

Agnathans: Jawless and covered with fine scales, many of the earliest fish had their heads encased in armoured shell of fused scales. They dominated the seas from the late Cambrian to the Devonian.

Almost all were small – under 30 centimetres long – and looked very odd, rather like a young child's drawing of a fish.

Placoderms: From the late Silurian to the early Carboniferous, the next type, the first fish with jaws, took over. Most of them lived on the sea-bed, as their flattened, armoured head and highly placed eyes indicate. Most were fairly small, but a few grew considerably larger – such as the monstrous, 9-metre-long Dunkleosteus!

Chondrichthyans: The 'true fish' of the Devonian Period came in two varieties, both of which are familiar to modern anglers. This class is for the sharks and rays, as they are more popularly known. All the fish in this class have skeletons made of cartilage rather than bone, so their remains are not as common as those of other fish types. However, sharks' teeth are very common fossils, because young sharks may grow a new tooth every day or two. Nowadays, we are justly wary of the Great White Shark; had we been around 400 million years ago, we would have been just as afraid of the 12-metre Carcharodon! Eek!

Osteichthyans: The other variety of fish is the bony fish from which most modern fish are descended. Their fossils come as teeth and bones and, occasionally, the impressions of scales in rocks. All modern fish are represented in the fossil record, but among them are some unusual types – including the Coelacanth, which is found in chalk deposits in Britain – some distance from Madagascar, where live samples of the Coelacanth turned up a few years ago!

Cetaceans: These are the whales, which aren't fish at all, we know – but, since we were talking about sea-creatures . . . They developed from land mammals which returned to the sea as recently as the Eocene Period. Prehistoric whales were very long and thin, only later gaining their modern bulk. Whale fossils are uncommon, but they are very impressive when they do turn up, as you can imagine.

SEA MONSTERS

Later, while dinosaurs roamed the Mesozoic landmasses, the sea was also home to giant monsters. These developed from small reptiles which returned to dwelling in the sea in the Triassic Period, rather like scaly versions of seals perhaps. Creatures like the various Ichthyosaurs and Plesiosaurs are famous as models for mythical sea-monsters. They were not fish and they had to surface to breathe in air, just like whales and dolphins. Although they are often grouped in with them, they are not strictly dinosaurs, though they are related to them.

Sea reptile fossils

Ichthyosaurs: Among the first fossil reptiles ever found and recognized by science, Ichthyosaurs were streamlined and dolphin-like, only with long snouts filled with teeth. Typically only a metre or so long, some grew up to five times that size.

Plesiosaurs: With its long neck and fatter, flipper-propelled body, the Plesiosaur is everyone's impression of the Loch Ness monster. (There's even been some suggestion that the mythical Scottish beastie is a pair of just such reptiles which were trapped by falling sea-levels millions of years ago. There is no proof of this; for the facts about Nessie, see *The UFO Investigator's Handbook*.)

Mosasaur: The largest of these slinky, almost croc-odile-like creatures grew to a whopping 10 metres in length. Their teeth and bones are fairly common in most parts of the world. They seem to have been quite aggressive predators; a fossil-hunter once found an ammonite that had had a huge chunk taken out of it by a Mosasaur's bite. Crunchy!

AMPHIBIANS

At the end of the Silurian Period, around the coasts of all the land-masses, fish and other creatures came up against the land. Eventually a few species began to venture out for short periods of time. Plants had made the move some 1 million years earlier. It is also possible that creatures like water scorpions had learnt to live on solid ground too.

However, the big development came when the first fish flopped out on to the mud and decided it rather liked life up there. Such creatures may have looked something like Chirodipterus, a relative of the modern lungfish – still equipped with gills and spending most of its life in the water, but also prone to wriggling up and basking on the land for a while.

Eventually the descendants of these creatures became skilled at living on land. They developed lungs to breathe air rather than water, though they still returned to the water to breed and lay their eggs. These amphibians were the first modern, land-dwelling creatures, and they are our very distant ancestors. These days, frogs and salamanders look much the same as they did way back in the Triassic Period.

Amphibian fossils

Eryops: A famous fossil of this massive, crocodile-shaped amphibian has been assembled and is on show at the Natural History Museum in London. Growing up to 2 metres in length, its remains are found in a number of Permian rock formations in the USA. It is heavily built, with strong bones and sharp teeth, suggesting it was a meat-eater.

Diplocaulus: Fossil remains of this curious, pond-dwelling amphibian have been found in Permian rock in Texas. It had a most peculiar, triangular, almost boomerang-shaped head that grew up to 40 centimetres across; this on a creature typically only 1 metre long). Investigators have suggested that its head may have acted like a hydrofoil to help keep the creature afloat in water – or as a deterrent to stop other creatures swallowing it (well, we wouldn't want to eat one).

REPTILES AND THEIR EGGS

The next big step – and it was a very large one, in hindsight – was the development of a miracle of natural engineering – the 'amniote egg'. This soft-shelled egg had its own fluids, and it enabled reptile babies to develop for a longer time, before being born, so their parents didn't have to return to the water for them to be born.

The first reptiles evolved in the Permian (which takes its name from the Perm region of the Ural Mountains, in Russia). The first reptiles were small, stunted-looking creatures, slightly resembling badly put-together lizards. Their legs splayed out on either side like a crocodile's do today. Slowly, however, different species evolved with their legs under their bodies, allowing them to move faster and have large, more powerful bodies. Eventually the reptiles developed into dinosaurs, but some became crocodiles, Pterosaurs and monstrous sea-creatures.

Fossil reptiles

Anapsids: Although this class includes the modern turtles and tortoises, its earlier members developed in the Carboniferous Period, as a series of shell-less, lizard-like creatures that had almost all died out by the time turtles evolved, 30 million years later. Bony turtle shells and skulls are fairly common fossils around the world.

Diapsids: The most common group of reptiles. Ignoring dinosaurs (we'll come to them in the next section, don't you worry), its main members are crocodiles, lizards and snakes. Diapsid fossils are typically found as skulls, teeth or vertebrae, in many locations all around the world.

Synapsids: Small, mammal-like reptiles first appeared during the Carboniferous. Early examples were slow and lizard-like, but they proved successful and developed many varieties. By the end of the Permian they were unable to compete for food and living space with the newly evolved dinosaurs and crocodiles. Their successors, the mammals, however, proved far more durable. Dimetrodon is the most famous of these reptiles, notable for the massive bony 'sail' on its back; several examples have been found in North America.

HERE ARE THE DINOSAURS!

The rise of the dinosaurs marked the beginning of the Mesozoic Era, starting with the Triassic Period. Originally they were almost exclusively small creatures, most being less than 30 centimetres long. Most of these early species were carnivorous but, interestingly, their direct descendants were the giant plant-eaters of the Jurassic Period. However, another strain developed from these early tiny proto-dinosaurs and evolved into the savage, fanged monsters we know and love today.

There were two main types of dinosaur. The *Saurischia* had grasping forefeet (which may have evolved into elephant-like feet, wings, etc.) and an s-shaped neck (though this would be very compressed in, say, a Tyrannosaurus). They were two- or four-footed, carnivorous or vegetarian; and they included within their number Tyrannosaurus rex, Diplodocus, Apatosaurus, Allosaurus, Oviraptor, Deinonychus and Velociraptor. Living alongside them were the *Ornithischia*. These were all plant-eaters, mostly four-footed, and all had either small teeth or none at the front, the latter sometimes replaced by a horny beak. Among their number are Ankylosaurus, Stegosaurus, Hadrosaurs (duck-billed dinosaurs) and the various Ceratopsids.

Dinosaur fossils are not exactly unknown, but they are pretty rare, worse luck. As a result, investigators have no real idea how many dinosaur species there were. Right at this moment, scientists believe that there are something over 10,000 different species of birds in the world – in comparison, from the whole of the late Cretaceous Period, we know of perhaps fifty dinosaur species!

The classic image of the dinosaur is of a rampaging carnivore or a slow, bumbling giant with a long neck. In fact, dinosaurs came in all shapes and sizes. The bird-like Compsognathus, for example, was about the size of a chicken and it probably tore about in a similarly raucous fashion (though perhaps without the clucking). Other dinosaurs, such as Velociraptor, were about the size of small lions (not the size of the monsters in the film *Jurassic Park*, sad to say). However, it's fair to say that the most breath-taking dinosaurs were the behemoths, the towering beasts and the lumbering giants.

Because they are the most fascinating of all fossils (and the type of fossils we all dream of finding), we'll look at the various types of dinosaur fossil in greater depth here – and tell you what different fossils can tell a dinosaur investigator about dinosaurs in return.

Dinosaur tracks and traces

'Trace fossils' can include trails, borings and bur-rows, droppings and other marks left behind by pre-historic creatures. Where we're talking about dinosaurs, however, this will almost always mean footprints!

Prints are found in all kinds of places around the world, from eastern Australia – where a set of Stegosaur footprints was actually stolen in 1996 – to England, scene of a very recent discovery of posi-tively ginormous prints from a herd of Diplodocuses (or is it Diplodoci?).

Tracks can be very impressive – imagine, a huge row of gigantic footprints that may stomp along for many metres. They may even have swishing marks near them, caused by the creature's tail. There is even a famous example that features just a set of front prints – the suggestion has been made that they were from a swimming dinosaur, pushing itself through the water using its front legs!

Footprints can tell us many special things about dinosaur behaviour. For example, we can work out the speed the creature was moving at. Complex models compare the length of the strides, the depth of the prints, the length of dinosaur legs and so on, to work out whether a creature was running in terror or strolling contentedly. The best recent evidence we have is that many dinosaurs, and especially the larger predators, were capable of quite a turn of speed

Tracks made by a dinosaur found in Texas, USA

if they needed it, especially over short distances!

Trackways which show the footprints of more than one dinosaur of the same sort are plainly evidence for new theories that some dinosaurs travelled in herds. A classic set of late Cretaceous tracks at Toro-Toro, in Bolivia, show the paths of six adults and two young. Both of the young are in the centre of the pack, between two adults. Just behind them, presumably shortly afterwards, came a pack of at least thirty-two medium-sized carnivorous dinosaurs, moving in the same direction. Hmm, wonder what they had for dinner?

Dinosaur eggs

All dinosaurs probably laid eggs. There's been some suggestion recently that a few species may have given birth to live young, but there is no conclusive evidence of this yet. In comparison, all modern birds and crocodiles lay eggs.

The famous Flaming Cliffs discoveries from the 1920s' expedition to Mongolia were only the first of many exciting discoveries of eggs. Another famous site is what has now been called Egg Mountain, in Montana, USA, where dozens of nests have been unearthed.

The eggs from Mongolia were about 18 centimetres long, with one end thinner than the other. The surfaces of all of the eggs were covered in small ridges. More importantly, all the eggs had been laid out in a pattern, with the narrow ends facing outwards, and then buried in the sand to keep them warm! This must mean that an adult dinosaur stuck around for a while after the eggs were laid, tending them, moving them to a good spot, and then scraping sand over them. Ahh!

At Egg Mountain, more interesting evidence was turned up. The bones of baby dinosaurs were found in the nests. Nothing too odd about that, sure – except that some of them had worn teeth, implying that they had stuck around for a few years before they died, and had been fed, which may have meant that their parents stayed around to feed them just like many birds do now!

Dinosaur teeth – and food

Carnivorous dinosaurs had sharp, serrated teeth, very like steak knives, for cutting up their prey. Early vegetarian dinosaurs had leaf-shaped teeth, which sliced together rather like shears or a pair of scissors, to cut away tough stalks. Later, some species developed a specially large block of teeth, composed of many dozens of individual units, that they used in order to grind up plants. And some dinosaurs, such as Oviraptor and Struthiomimus, didn't have any teeth at all, just a sharp, beak-like affair. Don't think that prevented them eating; after all, eagles don't have any teeth either.

Teeth, and the jaws they come in, can tell a clued-up dinosaur investigator a lot about what a particular species ate. Some jaws – such as those of a Tyrannosaur – were meant for closing round a prey and biting down hard. Their skulls often have large, open areas, which is where thick muscles were attached in order to power their enormous jaws. Others were for grabbing a thick branch and wrenching it free; Triceratops is a good example. Paradoxically, the hugest dinosaurs had some of the most delicate mouths – creatures like Apatosaurus just nibbled and chomped away on juicy leaves all day.

The Baryonyx found by Bill Walker, which we mentioned earlier, had a very unusual jaw: it was long and flattened, like a crocodile that's just been trodden on by a Diplodocus. Scientists are still studying it, but there have been suggestions that it used its mouth to grub through mud and shallow water in search of fish and small amphibians.

Skilled investigators can discover more about what a dinosaur might have eaten by looking in its stomach. Carnivorous dinosaurs have often been found with smaller bones inside them. In the stomach of a Coelophysis, a set of bones turned out to have come from a younger, um, Coelophysis. At first scientists thought that this might be because the dinosaur gave birth to live young, like a mammal, but the bones weren't small enough to belong to a baby – the creature was a cannibal dinosaur!

These days, ostriches and other birds swallow stones, which they keep in their stomachs or in a pouch in their throat in order to grind down tough vegetation before it can be digested. Such worn-down pebbles, called 'gastroliths', have also been found inside the stomachs of a number of vegetarian dinosaurs.

Dinosaur skin

Most of what we know about dinosaur skin has come from 'comparative studies' – that is, investigators have looked at similar modern creatures, such as crocodiles, and worked out that dinosaur skin must have been much the same. This has had to be done because, as we said before, it's usually only the hard, bony parts of a creature that get preserved when it is turned into a fossil.

But not always. A few spectacular fossils have turned up, complete with impressions of the scales from a dinosaur's skin. Probably the best is from a mummified Edmontosaurus which is in the American Museum of Natural History. It revealed that dinosaur skin was basically a complex array of scales, separated by flexible joints of thinner scales. Scientists imagine that it was similar to the skin birds have round their beaks and feet and under their feathers.

Some dinosaurs have very special skin which is embedded with small bones called 'osteoderms'. The Ankylosaurus is a classic example of this: it has a random array of bony plates set into most of its body.

So here's another question we asked earlier: what colour were dinosaurs? Well, to be truthful, no one knows. The colour always gets drained out of fossils, let alone those few rare finds of skin impressions. Some experts have said that they should be the colour of modern crocodiles and alligators – so that's brown or green. Others have pointed out that many birds have very bright plumage – and what about those beaded lizards from Mexico which come in wild purples and blacks and whites? At the moment no one knows for sure, and it's possible that this is one question which won't get answered because it's too hard to guess. After all, if experts had found a fossil zebra and did not have modern zebras to tell them its skin was of black and white stripes, would they have just compered it to a horse and said it must have been brown?

Dinosaur claws

Both meat- and plant-eating dinosaurs are known to have fought – though most of the time it was because the first lot were trying to kill and eat the second! A great many dinosaur bones have slash marks from old fights. One skull from a Tyrannosaurus found in South Dakota, USA, had a smashed-in eye and hundreds of scratches all over it – and a tooth from another Tyrannosaur stuck in it!

Fighting may also have been a way of proving dominance within herds or as a means of attracting a mate. The high, domed skulls of Pachycephalosaurs are 25 centimetres thick. There is the implication that they fought one another by butting heads, just like rams fighting for the leadership of a herd.

Dinosaur bones

Even though some species of dinosaur were unquestionably the biggest animals ever to roam across the

Palaeontologists in Niger, West Africa, strengthening a Sauropod dinosaur bone with plaster so they can move it

Earth, they all had round about the same number of bones as any other vertebrate. In all creatures, be it bat, bird or Barosaurus, the basic structure of the skeleton is the same.

This is a great help in allowing us to identify unfamiliar bones. Even our own bodies have bones that are very similar in shape to those in, say, an Iguanodon. Only a few dinosaurs have more bones than normal – and these are to be found in the extremely long tails of mighty beasts like Diplodocus.

Dinosaurs, we know, come in different sizes. We can work out the weights of dinosaurs by working out how tall and wide they were, because for every creature, a cubic centimetre of their body weighs about one gram, a fact which is dead handy.

The longest dinosaur known to science (so far) was Seismosaurus, at 40–52 metres in length. It could also prove to have been even heavier than the previous record-holder, Brachiosaurus, which is estimated by some to have weighed somewhere between 30 and 50 tonnes! (Compare this to your average 5.4-tonne elephant, then go 'Wow!')

In contrast, some of the smallest dinosaurs ever were about the same size as small dogs or large birds. Compsognathus longus, a bird-like dinosaur from the early Jurassic, was about 70 centimetres in length, including a long tail, and it weighed only about 3 kilos. That's lighter than your average school-bag of a morning. The only problem with small dinosaurs is that their bones can prove very fragile, and so are rarely found. It may well be that there were far more small dinosaurs than monstrously large ones; we just haven't found evidence of their passing yet.

Hot or cold?

Bones can also give us a lot of information about the inner workings of a dinosaur. The Big Question to do with bones is whether they can be used to determine whether dinosaurs were warm- or cold-blooded, which in turn may help with working out why they are all extinct (so it's a pretty important question). The famous palaeontologist Robert Bakker is a leading researcher in this field.

Birds are warm-blooded (or, more properly,

'endothermic'). That is, their temperature is raised or lowered internally to match their environment. Crocodiles and lizards are cold-blooded ('ectothermic'). They have to use external means, such as lying in the sun to warm up or lying in the shade to cool down. For the most part, cold-blooded creatures move more slowly than hot-blooded ones, and they could not live in very changeable climates.

So which were the dinosaurs? To find out, scientists have been taking ultra-thin slices through bones. (Yes, we know, what a waste of a good dinosaur skeleton.) Slicing through bones in this manner can, under a fine microscope, sometimes reveal a structure that should indicate whether the creature was cold- or warm-blooded.

The trouble is, dinosaur bones are so old and are usually turned to stone by fossilization, so it's very hard to tell which sort the dinosaurs were. Obviously there are also other factors from dinosaur behaviour that can influence the conclusion, but the jury are still out on this one.

FILE STATUS

The debate about whether dinosaurs were hot- or cold-blooded continues to rage, with arguments on both sides. It is suspected that some primitive, bird-like dinosaurs were cold-blooded, unlike their modern descendants. Meanwhile, some earlier dinosaurs do appear to have been warm-blooded. The debate goes on!

DINOSAURS TAKE OFF!

The first creatures to fly were insects. Huge dragonflies buzzed and swooped among the ferns as far back as 300 mya. However, when reptiles became the dominant class of creatures on the land, it was only a matter of time before one group of them literally started to take off.

Strictly speaking, the Pterosaurs of the Mesozoic Era are not dinosaurs but a related group of reptiles. Whatever they are, however, they are pretty alarming creatures, with their wide, leathery wings stretching from their vastly elongated, extended fourth fingers, and their strangely shaped, streamlined heads. Take a look at this Pteranodon, a member of the Pterosaur group.

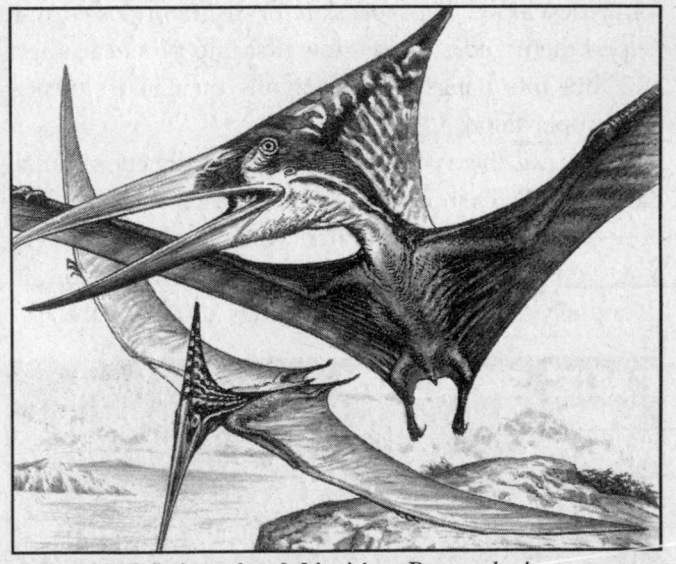

Is it a bird? Is it a plane? No, it's a Pteranodon!

Totally separate from the pterosaurs, a whole new class of dinosaur developed in the Jurassic: the birds. Once thought of as a line distinct from the dinosaurs, it is now plain that modern birds are, in fact, real paid-up members of the dinosaur family!

How flight developed

There are two very simple-to-understand rival theories about flight that continue to have the scientists arguing till they're blue in the face. They are the 'Trees Down' and the 'Ground Up' theories, and support for both seems evenly matched.

The first says that some small and light-boned dinosaurs lived up in the branches, where they became adept at hopping from branch to branch. Eventually some developed flaps of skin or feathery scales that helped them glide. These grew first into proper feathers and thus into wings, and eventually their glides turned into proper flight.

The rival theory works in the other direction. Small dinosaurs like Deinonychus ran on two legs, chasing their prey. As they ran, they jumped and hopped. Feathery scales evolved to allow them to stay airborne longer. Eventually they developed into wings and learned to fly.

FILE STATUS

More facts are needed. There have been recent discoveries of some hotly disputed remains of dinosaurs which appeared to run on their hind legs but which had feathery skins; keep alert for more information.

Fossil flyers

Pterosaurs: The largest of the Pterosaurs, the Pteranodon of the Cretaceous Period, grew until it had a wingspan of up to 7 metres – which is wider than many light aircraft! It appears to have been a fish-eater which soared over the oceans like an albatross on the air currents, or it made its nest on cliffs to help it take off and land. In other parts of the world, according to evidence found in Kazakhstan, small Pterodactyls developed light fur, presumably to keep out the cold. All Pterosaur fossils are fairly rare.

Archaeopteryx: This is one of the most famous fossil creatures ever found. Palaeontologists have only ever discovered six Archaeopteryx fossils, and only two have the impressions of feathers on them. The creature was chicken-sized, with a toothed beak (unlike a modern bird) and feathered wings and tail. Some dinosaur investigators have questioned whether it even flew at all; it is possible that it just ran along the ground, feeding on insects and small reptiles.

Aepyornis: Also known as the elephant bird, the fossils of this ostrich-shaped giant have been found in Madagascar. It grew to a staggering height of 4 metres and may have weighed as much as 450 kilos. Just imagine trying to get through that for Christmas lunch.

AND FINALLY THE MAMMALS

Although we've placed them last on the list, the earliest mammals actually developed at around the same time as the early dinosaurs. Way back then, they were small and shrew-like, and they had little impact on the ecology. Once those big leathery reptiles had all mysteriously popped their clogs, however, the mammals set about developing and multiplying like nobody's business. At first, marsupials (which nurture their young in pouches) were more populous than placentals (those which give birth to live young). In Australia, where there was little competition, marsupials still thrive.

Elsewhere, however, the mammals developed into the creatures that populate the rest of the world today. In the Eocene Period, mammals with hoofs developed, and soon after came the large carnivores. There were a few evolutionary dead-ends, including giant species of many creatures that are still around today. One fascinating example is the sabre-toothed cats, such as Hoplophoneous, from the Oligocene, with its 25-centimetre-long front teeth. Just imagine having to brush those every morning.

Mammal fossils

Early mammals: Extinct species such as the insect-eating Amblotherium and Taeniolabis looked like small shrews or rodents. Their bones were light and small, and many are known only through their teeth, so making them rare finds.

Glyptodon: This oddly endearing-looking South American creature was the large (2-metre-long) fore-runner of the modern armadillo, but it had an all-over, almost spherical, armoured shell.

Mammuthus: The common mammoth, from the Pleistocene, may have been hunted by early man. They were smaller than full-grown African elephants, and were covered in thick red-brown hair as a protection from the cold. Whole carcasses have been found preserved in ice, matching images in European cave-paintings.

Megatherium: Only found in Argentina, this massive sloth measured up to 6 metres in length! Luckily for its neighbours, it was a vegetarian.

Paraceratherium: This huge creature, often measuring more than 5 metres at the shoulder, was among the largest land mammals ever to have lived. Imagine a gigantic, long-legged, hornless rhino. It lived on leaves from the tops of trees, and its bones have been found in Europe and Asia.

Where Did They All Go?

Of all the Big Questions regarding dinosaurs, this is the biggest of the big. We know that dinosaurs aren't around nowadays. So they must have died out. A look at the fossil record confirms this. In rocks up to 65 million years old, dinosaur bones, if not exactly plentiful, are found on a regular basis. After that date, nothing! They've simply gone, died out, extinct.

It seems that, at the end of the Cretaceous Period, there was a mass extinction. Many creatures simply died out. Among them were the dinosaurs, Pterosaurs, various sea-dwelling reptiles, some lizards – and some surprising creatures, too, such as all of the ammonites. Now, because we aren't able to measure time exactly, we don't know whether they were all wiped out in a week or over 20,000 years. All we know is that they died, species after species.

As you can imagine, palaeontologists have come up with a wide variety of theories for the great extinction. Some of these are decidedly odd, while others are merely far-fetched, but the bottom line is simple: something wiped out the dinosaurs but left other creatures, including mammals and birds, still alive to take over the surface of the planet.

In trying to answer this Big Question, every single dinosaur investigator has a part to play. No one knows where the proof will come from. It could even come from a small, apparently insignificant fossil found by an amateur, out fossil-hunting for enjoyment. Keep your wits about you: you could find the answer.

Here are some of the many theories put forward to explain the decline of the dinosaurs.

Atchooo!: This theory suggests that they got hay fever from newly evolved Cretaceous flowering plants. Ahem. Taking this somewhat unlikely theory seriously for a moment, it has been pointed out that birds and crocodiles, species related to the dinosaurs that didn't die out, are not known to suffer from hay fever. However, this one probably doesn't explain the extinction of other species, such as the sea-dwelling ammonites. (Besides which, to be honest, it's a pretty daft theory.)

Who ate all the pies?: Another theory puts it bluntly: dinosaurs just grew too big! They hit an evolutionary dead-end, and died out. Well, we know that, at the end of the Cretaceous, among the dinosaurs were the largest animals ever to have walked on land. However, dinosaurs that were almost as large existed millions of years previously, in the Mesozoic, and there were no extinctions then. Also, it has to be said that all the dinosaurs died out, both big and small.

Who ate all the eggs?: According to this theory, those pesky varmints, the mammals, out-competed the dinosaurs for the available food and slowly starved them out through sheer weight of numbers.

A variant suggests that the mammals could have eaten all the dinosaurs' eggs, slowly reducing their numbers as fewer and fewer baby dinosaurs were born. This one is especially hard to prove or disprove. However, the fossil record does not show a marked increase in the number of mammals just before the dinosaurs died out; it was only after the dinosaurs had departed that the mammals diversified and became the dominant species. Besides, dinosaurs managed to live alongside plentiful numbers of primitive mammals for over 100 million years without any food problems.

Brrrr, it's a bit nippy!: As we know, the level of the seas changed constantly. During the dinosaurs' heyday in the Cretaceous Period, large shallow seas had spread over many of the continents. These kept the weather fairly stable: the summers not too hot, the winters not too cold; days weren't too warm, and nights not too cool. However, changes in the sea level could have changed the climate and killed off the cold-blooded dinosaurs.

What proof is there for this? Well, we know that at the end of the Cretaceous, as the geological record goes some way towards proving, the seas retreated. Over a period of about 100,000 years, temperatures veered wildly and the climate became more extreme. Different parts of the globe now had markedly different weather.

There are many plausible parts to this theory, but ultimately it's not enough to explain the extinction of the dominant species of the entire planet. Also, it is now thought that some dinosaurs may have been warm-blooded. Furthermore, if the dinosaurs were finished off by the temperature, surely other related creatures, such as crocodiles, would have gone as well?

Cough! Cough!: As well as the aforementioned change in sea levels, the end of the Cretaceous saw a tremendous increase in volcanic activity around the world; for example, lava buried the whole of India. Huge explosions in the southern Atlantic and the middle of America hurled ash over most of the world. It is likely that such explosions also released clouds of sulphurous gas into the atmosphere, causing acid rain and the poisoning of the sea. Under the thick ash clouds there would be little direct sunlight, and the temperature would have dropped dramatically.

It's a grim picture, and there is some credibility in it. However, under such apocalyptic conditions, surely everything would have died, not just the dinosaurs? Now, maybe the other species managed to evolve fast enough for enough numbers to survive this period, but there is no proof of this from the fossil record – at least, not yet.

Ker-smash!: Having exhausted all the current theories, scientists kept looking for further clues to the extinction. Returning to the scene of the crime, as it were, they re-examined the rocks from 65 million years ago – and they found something very important.

Between the last layer of rock from the end of the Cretaceous Period and that starting the Cenozoic Era, there's a thin bed of clay. While they were testing this to see how long it took to be deposited, the experts found it possessed far too much of a very special ingredient: *iridium*!

This element usually exists in a metallic state, so it is most commonly found in the Earth's core, and also on meteorites. Under normal conditions it would have taken a million years of meteor falls to leave as much iridium as was in that thin layer – but the soil was laid down, tests revealed, in a far shorter time.

So how did that (comparatively great amount of) iridium get there? Here's one theory: a single gigantic meteor or asteroid, about 10–15 kilometres across, smashed into the Earth. The resulting fall-out of fragments and dust thrown all round the world laid down all that iridium. The impact from that immense collision raised a dust-cloud which cut off all sunlight for several months. Surface temperatures dropped below freezing. Plants became stunted. Extensive acid-rain followed. In the long term, as a result of the greenhouse effect, the world's temperature rose. In the resulting upheaval, only those creatures which could adapt quickly survived – and that didn't include the dinosaurs. But again, is it likely that they all died out and left so many other species behind?

There are some other problems with this theory. For example, iridium is also thrown out by volcanoes

– and we already know there were more of those blowing their tops around this time. In support of the asteroid theory, though, there are also smaller traces of rarer elements such as osmium in the same clay layer, and that is not thrown out by an erupting volcano.

A thought struck many dinosaur investigators when they heard about this theory. Something that big would leave a pretty hefty dent on the Earth's surface. So where was it? For many years, no one knew. Some geologists suggested it might be buried very deep or have been destroyed by subsequent volcanic and Continental Drift activity.

However, in 1991, a serious candidate was discovered – the Chicxulub crater on the Yucatan Peninsula in the Gulf of Mexico, in Central America. It's positively enormous, with an estimated diameter of 175 kilometres or more. And how old is it? Well, the sophisticated dating of melted rock inside the crater itself suggests that it may be around 65 million years old, give or take 50,000 years. (Cue a roomful of scientists snapping their fingers, punching their palms, going 'Aha!' and so on.)

At the moment, the asteroid theory is the one attracting the most attention. Many palaeontologists are right behind it; others, however, continue to point out all the flaws. It may well be that what in fact happened was a mixture of all of them: the dinosaurs were frozen, choked, starved and ultimately smashed out of existence! More information is needed; more dinosaurs are needed for study . . . which is where you come in.

FILE STATUS

No single theory has yet been proved.
More information urgently needed.

Out in the Field

If you're going to go off on a fossil hunt – and if you have the opportunity, it can be tremendous fun – you'll need some special tools. Luckily, if all you are doing is wandering along near the bottom of a cliff or escarpment looking for loose fragments, there is little you'll need other than a couple of large pockets in which to put any fossils you find. If you are a little more serious about fossil-hunting, however, there are other items of equipment, from the everyday to the very complicated.

Luckily, the most important pieces of equipment you will need as an investigator are ones you've already got: your brain and your senses. With these you'll be able to look out for the right rock strata, find clues to the presence of fossils, and hopefully track some down. Fossil-hunters walk slowly, scanning gullies, cliffs or piles of weathered fragments at the bottom of slopes. Patience may be needed if you are to find anything truly spectacular – but it can be incredibly rewarding when you do. Get into the habit of keeping your eyes and ears open for anything out of the ordinary. As you add more and more fossils to your collection, you will become more skilled at finding them and explaining their presence.

Tools you can trust

We've already mentioned the usefulness of geological maps of an area to a fossil-hunter. You can find maps in your local library – but make sure they are up to date. There's no point in trekking halfway across the county to check out a promising-looking escarpment, only to find an eight-lane bypass thundering over it. Your local natural history group may have more up-to-date information.

Always carry a notebook and pens; make sure they are sturdy enough to survive being carried around, and use waterproof inks so your notes won't go all soggy if you are unlucky enough to get rained on. Use your notebook to record the type of rock formation, the location of a find, the circumstances of a find, sketches of items before they were dug out or taken away, and more sketches of the items themselves. Basically, get into the habit of keeping notes; you never know when you might need them.

A camera could also come in handy for recording a find. A light, cheap model will do for most purposes. Just remember to keep your thumb out of the viewfinder and to carry enough film to take all the shots you need.

If you find an important fossil, a compass and a tape-measure will allow you to record the exact spot where you made your find. This may prove especially important if you want to come back and do some more digging in order, say, to find the rest of the creature that the brand-new claw belongs to . . .

Some fossils are very small, so you'll find a small, fold-up hand-lens or a magnifying glass will come in handy for peering at tiny details.

On the other hand, you may also find large nodular stones that you suspect could contain fossils. These can be split up by using a special broad-bladed chisel called a bolster, providing you use it along the grain of the rock.

Digging in

If you are lucky enough to come across a fossil still embedded in a cliff or rock formation, you may want to attempt to extract it. Before you start, ensure that an adult is with you and that you have permission. Make sure you are safe, that you are wearing the right safety gear, that you are not doing anything prohibited and that you really do want to spend the next however-many-hours digging and chiselling away. After all, there may be just as good fossils lying all round you in the debris.

When you are digging, be gentle, work away slowly. If in doubt, leave the fossil where it is rather than damage it trying to gouge it out in a hurry. Most likely, it'll still be there another day.

If a fossil really is too big to dig out, make a very detailed record in your notebook of where it can be found, and call in some real experts from your local museum or natural history society.

There is a special type of geological hammer which can be very useful for digging out rocks; it has one blunt end and one sharp one. It can be expensive, though, so make sure you are really keen on fossil-hunting before you splash out on one. You may also need a selection of chisels for chipping away solid rock. Make sure you get the ones with guarded handles; these stop your from getting smashed fingers if you miss the end with your hammer in all the excitement.

For extracting small or delicate fossils from soft rock, you may need only a brush, or possibly a trowel or small spade. Trowels or small spades are better for removing softer sediment, especially sand. A small sieve will allow you to separate tiny fossil fragments such as teeth and small bones from dust and mud. A range of different-sized meshes will allow you to trap different-sized fossils, of course. If you're in a hurry on a dig, gather up samples of loose rock for sieving through when you get home; given the time to take it steady, you may find many tiny fossil teeth, bones or seeds that you could miss out in the field.

If you manage to find some fossils, you'll need to get them home. Small plastic pots or sandwich boxes are usually enough for smaller fossils. Larger fossils can go in a sturdy bag. As a general common-sense rule, if it's too heavy for your bag, leave it for some other poor fool to stagger off with – unless you're sure it really is a Triceratops head or Brachiosaur femur, of course.

Important: If you are digging anywhere near a cliff, or in loose piles of rock that may be sharp, you must wear safety gear. Gloves will protect your hands from scratches and bruises. Safety goggles will keep flying chips of rock from blinding you. A safety helmet will protect your head – but remember that it won't help you in the event of a large rock-fall. If in doubt, go and look for fossils somewhere else.

Preparing a fossil

As you will quickly learn, fossil-collecting isn't just about digging the things out. When you get your fossils home – this is assuming you find any, of course – you will need to prepare them for your collection.

First, wash the dust off then clean away any dirt and debris. If a fossil still has some rock stuck to it, you will need to use a brush or a scraping tool to remove it. A heavy darning needle will be enough to remove small fragments; for larger lumps of rock, many amateur fossil-collectors use dental instruments bought from medical suppliers.

In a museum, a professional dinosaur-restorer might use a very gentle acid to remove stray lumps of rock from round a fossil. However, we don't recommend that you try this on your own. If you want or need to do this, go to an acknowledged expert – let *them* make a dreadful mess rather than you!

If a fossil is cracked or broken, you should be able to glue it together easily enough – but remember to use a glue that can be removed again later on if you need to reposition the pieces. In the past, people have varnished fossils to protect them from knocks and chips. This is fine if you want to turn a fossil sea-urchin into a handy paperweight (a lovely gift for a grandparent or a favourite uncle), but it can clog up all the fine detail. If you store your fossils carefully, they should be safe enough.

Building a collection

Put your fossils in shallow trays or in the lids of small cardboard boxes, then put the whole lot in a drawer. As well as keeping them all in one place and out of harm's way, it will mean they're not out on shelves gathering lots of dust.

If you have any particularly small specimens, a better way to store them might be on microscope cavity slides, held in place by water-soluble glue or secured beneath a transparent cover glass.

Make a label for each fossil in your collection, recording as much detail as you can. This should include the following:

> *Name of the fossil*
> *Name of the creature it's from, if you know it*
> *The rock it was found in*
> *That rock's geological age*
> *The place where you found it, including a map reference and the county*
> *The date you found it*

If you have room on the back, keep further notes about what happened when you found it and any theories you may have about it. Also keep a record of any special glues, varnish or other odd materials you used in preparing or restoring your fossil. Maybe, just maybe, if it turns out to be a truly important find, museum staff will need to know just what gunk they will have to scrape off it in order to restore it properly!

Keep a back-up of all your labels as computer files, so you can refer to them at a later date. Using your computer, compare different specimens of the same type, or different fossils from the same location. See if you can come up with any theories as to why such fossils came to be where you found them. Who knows: if you set your mind to it, you may come up with some pretty startling theories of your own.

Erm, Are You Sure About That?

You'd think it was easy, wouldn't you? You dig around among the right rocks, until you come to something that plainly isn't just stone. *Voilà*, you've found a fossil. But even the experts make mistakes, sometimes quite big ones, in identifying what they thought were fossils or dinosaur bones. However, we're confident that you won't make that sort of mistake . . .

Natural formations

Flint is a strange rock. Although it usually comes as large, rounded pebbles, on occasions it can turn up in far more deceptive shapes. In the past, people have knocked on the doors of museums carrying flints shaped like ducks' heads, noses, shrunken heads, legs, fingers, and many more. Oh dear.

Trickier to spot is banded flint. This is laid down in bands and is sometimes found folded round itself so that it looks as if it's made of tiny tubes. Give it a little staining, weather it a little in an exposed position, and it's a dead ringer for a fossil wormcast, a mollusc or, especially, a cluster of coral.

Less commonly, when the element manganese seeps into a porous rock it can often spread out in branching rivulets that look very much like the divisions in a fossil plant. These formations, called dendrites, have deceived even the wariest of experts.

The Iguanodon's horn

Back when palaeontology was in its infancy and dinosaurs were strange and new, mistakes in interpreting the fragmentary fossil remains recovered from the earth were rife.

One of the most distinctive features of the Iguanodon is the large, spike-shaped thumb that sits upright from its small fore-limbs. When its bones were first discovered, however, it was suggested by the famous Richard Owen, following the ideas of Georges Cuvier, that the creature was a reptilian form of rhinoceros! He thought that it might have walked on four legs, with the spike perched proudly on the end of its snout. Indeed, initial sketches and models were constructed along just such lines. However, common sense prevailed and the thumbs were restored to their proper place before the turn of the century.

Many other mistakes have been made over the years. Since many of the apparently complete skeletons in museum displays today are actually from five or more examples of the same creature, it is rather more common than it should be for a museum to stick the wrong head or another part on to a totally different skeleton.

Remember the 'Dinosaur Wars' between Edward Drinker Cope and Othniel Marsh at the turn of the century? Their great rivalry started before then, back in 1870. The young Cope, eager to get one over on the other scholar, proudly showed Marsh the skeleton of an Elasmosaurus that he had reconstructed. The other scientist walked round it for a moment, studying it – and then, peering closer, he pointed out that Cope had stuck the head on the wrong end!

Mistakes still happen, though sometimes the errors can actually help rather than hinder investigations. In Germany in 1973, some scientists were re-examining the complete skeleton of a small, two-legged dinosaur which had been identified as a Compsognathus. Again they must have peered a little closer – for it eventually became apparent that it was, in fact, an Archaeopteryx in all its glory (though without any feather impressions). In this case, the mistaken identity set the scientists thinking about how similar ground-based dinosaurs were to the flying varieties; perhaps the two were closely related?

On the other hand, errors can sometimes create entirely the wrong impression about a dinosaur. Out in Mongolia, at the famous Flaming Cliffs digs of the 1920s, investigators found Protoceratops bones and, near by, a whole cluster of eggs in nests, which were assumed to be from the Protoceratops. The insides of these eggs had turned to stone, so it was impossible to see what was inside them. A little later, in a few nests, they went on to find the bones of a smaller, apparently sneakier dinosaur. They called it Oviraptor, which means 'egg-stealer'. And so we all came to believe in the happy little scenes shown in books and reconstructed in museums of Protoceratops babies hatching merrily out of their eggs.

When American palaeontologists returned to the Flaming Cliffs in the 1990s, they found some far better-preserved nests – complete with fossil Oviraptors plainly sitting on them to keep the eggs warm so they would hatch. Far from being egg thieves, it seems that the Oviraptors were very proper parents!

The Oviraptor, no longer labelled an egg thief

Visiting Dinosaurs

The best places to see dinosaurs in all their glory are, of course, museums. You may have thought that these were desperately dull and dusty places, full of nothing but old coins and bits of broken pottery. However, many are packed with fascinating fossils and reconstructed dinosaurs. These days they may also have fully working animatronic reconstructions and other incredible attractions. There's a general law for museums: the larger the city, the better the range of fossils and dinosaurs in their museum.

Britain

The following museums have permanent displays of dinosaurs. They are all well worth a visit. Also keep an eye out for special visiting exhibitions of, for example, the newest Chinese dinosaurs. Many other local museums will feature a selection of lesser fossils from the surrounding area.

Birmingham: Department of Natural History, Birmingham Museum – dinosaurs, many fossils
Cambridge: Sedgwick Museum, Cambridge University – dinosaurs, fossils
Cardiff: National Museum of Wales – large collection of fossils
Dorchester: The Dinosaur Museum – dinosaurs, tracks, fossils
Edinburgh: Royal Scottish Museum – dinosaurs, early fossils

Elgin: Elgin Museum – fossils from early Mesozoic

Glasgow: Hunterian Museum, Glasgow University – Triceratops skull, many fossils

Leicester: Leicestershire Museum and Art Gallery – disputed new dinosaur, local fossils

London: British Museum (Natural History) – The Natural History Museum is the first stop for anyone wanting to see an incredible array of permanent displays of dinosaurs and other fossils. Look out for special visiting exhibitions, such as the latest finds from China.

Lyme Regis: Lyme Regis Museum – Ichthyosaurs and other sea creatures, fossils

Manchester: Manchester Museum – thousands of fossils and geological exhibits

Newcastle: Hancock Museum – wide variety of fossils, and a big geological section too

Oxford: University Museum – many dinosaurs and wide variety of fossils

Portsmouth: Cumberland House Natural Science Museum – fossils and several Ichthyosaurs

Sandown, Isle of Wight: Museum of Isle of Wight Geology – local fossils, many dinosaur parts

Sunderland: Sunderland Museum – Permian fossils, fish and reptiles

York: Yorkshire Museum – fossils, extinct birds

Other famous museums

OK, so you're off on your hols . . . just for once, perhaps getting dragged round a museum may not be quite as dull as usual . . .

Australia: Australian Museum, Sydney; Queensland Museum, Brisbane; South Australian Museum, Adelaide

Austria: Natural History Museum, Vienna

Belgium: Bernissart Museum, Bernissart (especially for fans of Iguanodons!); Institut Royal des Sciences Naturelles de Belgique, Brussels

Canada: National Museum of Natural Sciences, Ottawa; Royal Ontario Museum, Toronto; Tyrell Museum of Paleontology, Drumheller, Alberta

France: National Museum of Natural History, Paris

Germany: Natural History Museum, Berlin; Senckenberg Nature Museum, Frankfurt; State Museum for Natural History, Stuttgart

India: Geology Museum, Indian Statistical Institute, Calcutta

Italy: Museo Civico di Storia Naturala di Venezia, Venice; Museum of Palaeontology, Institute of Geology and Palaeontology, Rome

Japan: Museum of Natural History, Osaka; National Science Museum, Tokyo

Poland: Institute of Palaeobiology, Warsaw

South Africa: Bernard Price Institute of Palaeontology, Johannesburg; South African Museum, Cape Town

Spain: Natural Science Museum, Madrid

Sweden: Palaeontological Museum, Uppsala

USA: American Museum of Natural History, New York; Carnegie Museum of Natural History, Pittsburgh; Dinosaur National Monument, Jensen, Utah; Los Angeles County Museum, Los Angeles;

National Museum of Natural History (The Smithsonian), Washington, DC

Real-life Dinosaurs

Of course, if you really want to visit some dinosaurs, what better way than to go and look at some that are still alive?

Modern dinosaurs

If you want to see a dinosaur right now, go and look out of the window. Go on, try it. See them all? No? 'Course you do! Look at all those little dinosaurs, the ones with the feathers and the beaks, sitting in the trees and on the fence. Yes, as we said earlier, birds aren't just related to dinosaurs, they are actually members of the same family of creatures. They really are genuine dinosaurs, albeit without the long necks, the five-tonne bodies or the twenty-centimetre teeth. Somehow, though, birds just aren't the same.

Naturalists refer to some creatures as 'living fossils'. This means that they evolved into their current form a very long time ago – and then stayed in it for millions of years. In effect, they are old-fashioned, in an evolutionary sense, fossils even.

Some of these creatures are distinctly mundane. Sharks and rays, with their odd, cartilage-stuffed bodies, are one example. Cockroaches are another; they've outlived the dinosaurs and will probably see us off too, without a single design modification.

More exotically, consider that little joke by Mother

Nature, the duck-billed platypus. It's a furry mammal (or, more correctly, a marsupial), yet it has webbed duck's feet, a duck-like bill and it lays eggs! When the first examples were brought back to London late in the eighteenth century by early settlers, naturalists thought they were a complete fake! We now know that the creature developed a very long time ago – perhaps as the first step down an evolutionary path that was never followed any further.

The most famous of all living fossils is, of course, the Coelacanth. This odd-looking fish, with its distinctive three-lobed tail and front fins which attach to its body with shoulder-like joints, was thought to have become extinct in the Cretaceous Period. At least, that is, until December 1938, when a live one

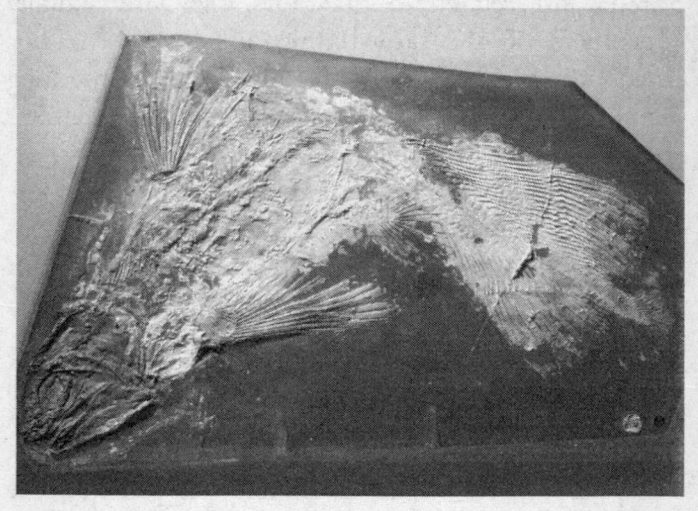

A fossil Coelacanth – try fishing for one of these next time you're by the sea

was caught by a fisherman off Madagascar. Further specimens have since been caught and some living examples have been photographed and filmed in very deep water (up to 400 metres down) off the Comoro Islands, north-east of Madagascar.

Living proof?

When one thinks of the Coelacanth, an extremely ancient creature that has somehow managed to survive exactly as it was at the time of the dinosaurs, one of those Big Questions keeps coming up. Here it is: is it possible that proper dinosaurs could have survived, in some extremely remote part of the world? Could there really be dinosaurs still alive today?

The brief answer is simple: a great big no. We have no proof that any have survived. Apart from that stuff with the birds, there have been no confirmed discoveries of any dinosaur found anywhere on this planet. Of course, that doesn't stop people reporting a Plesiosaur in Loch Ness, a Diplodocus in the Congo, a Mosasaur off Cornwall, Pterodactyls in Montana, and many more. But so far all these 'sightings' have been unproven, and may be as much wishful thinking as UFOs and ghosts.

However, it is just possible that, given that we have not explored all of the ocean, there could be other creatures, other 'living fossils' like the Coelacanth, hidden down in the depths.

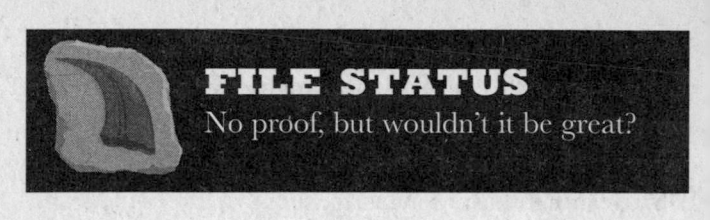

FILE STATUS
No proof, but wouldn't it be great?

Can we rebuild them?

Because of *Jurassic Park*, the last Big Question always seems to be followed by another one. You can probably guess it: can we, or will we be soon be able to, re-create dinosaurs from their DNA?

Well, it's a idea that is being taken very seriously by some scientists. What they have found, though, is that, because the DNA from any creature is such a hugely fragile substance and one that decomposes easily and dissolves in water, it will be preserved in fossils only under the most incredibly lucky circumstances.

What about a part of a dinosaur preserved in amber, like in the book and the movie? It's possible. DNA from insects that were imprisoned in their sticky tomb in the late Cretaceous Period has allegedly been isolated. However, on the entire planet, there has only ever been one piece of amber found with a single dinosaur part preserved in it – and that's a feather.

Even if dinosaur DNA is found and extracted, a huge advance still needs to be made before we can grow our own Jurassic Park. We can't grow anything from DNA yet. Our first successful experiments at cloning were reported only in early 1997, and they needed the presence of a living original to work from.

Doing all the maths about how likely this all is, then . . . well, let's just say you wouldn't want to bet your life on it.

However, the very latest news is that scientists in Montana may have managed to obtain some genuine dinosaur molecules. How? Not by using a fossilized fly, as in the *Jurassic Park* method, but by using a very well-preserved Tyrannosaurus rex bone. Various biochemicals, including proteins, have been extracted from the bone, and the scientists are all very excited about it. This news is hot off the press, so nobody knows whether all this research will one day produce some real dinosaur DNA. But don't hold your breath!

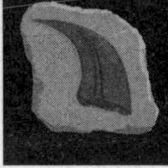

FILE STATUS

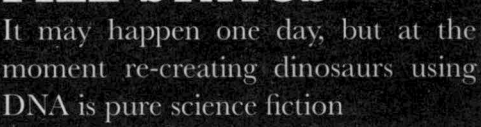

It may happen one day, but at the moment re-creating dinosaurs using DNA is pure science fiction

Field Support for Investigators

As you will have come to realize, truly dedicated dinosaur investigators are pioneers. Out in the field every day, come rain or shine, they stop at nothing to track down the latest fossils. OK, well, maybe not when it's raining. Or when it's too cold to hold a geologist's hammer. But you know what we mean. Grr!

However, fossil-collecting can also be a very social hobby, an excuse to have a lot of fun out in the open air and just maybe help to explain the entire history of the Earth along the way. As a result, there are some groups which investigators can turn to for help along the way.

Here are some handy resources which may come in very useful during your continuing investigations.

The Dinosaur Society

The Dinosaur Society is a large organization for people interested in dinosaurs; it was founded in America in 1991. Its aims are to encourage the study of dinosaurs round the world. Among its members are dinosaur scientists, authors, artists – and many amateur investigators. As well as offering funding for many expeditions and digs, the society passes on news and information about the latest developments in the field. In 1994 it set up a British branch, The Dinosaur Society UK. It even has its own magazine for young dinosaur-hunters, *DinoMite*. Drop them a line and ask for more information about what they can offer members, and how much it currently costs to join.

Contact: The Dinosaur Society UK, PO Box 329, Canterbury, Kent CT4 5GB

E-mail: jkb22@tutor.open.ac.uk

Museums

Most large towns and cities have a local museum dedicated to the town and its surrounding area. If your part of the world is especially rich in dinosaur finds, there may also be a permanent display of dinosaurs or fossils (see the list of major collections earlier).

If you have any queries about what you have found, one way of getting an expert's opinion is to take your finds to your local museum and ask for advice. If they can't help you, they will know a man who can.

Your local museum will also be able to tell you if there is a local fossil-hunting or a general natural history club. If there is, consider joining, They may well organize fossil hunts and dinosaur digs, and allow you access to sites that members of the public can't ordin-arily visit. Of course, a club may also put on interminably boring talks and slide-shows on the most tedious of subjects, but we're sure you'll be able to avoid those meetings.

Further reading

A dedicated investigator will know his or her subject inside out. Typically, because dinosaurs are such popular creatures, there are a great many books about them clogging up the shelves of bookshops and libraries. However, working on the assumption that you can never have too much information, we've read most of them.

Some books are far too complicated or obscure for any but the nerdiest dino expert to enjoy, while others are rip-offs of the 'Here's some pretty piccies of the lickle dinosaurs; that'll be twenty quid' variety. Ever helpful, however, we've chucked those ones out and have found the best to help you.

We've divided the list into General titles, which are suitable for anyone with the slightest interest in the subject, and Specialist, which are for boffins, brain-boxes and anyone who is really, really into dinosaurs (so you'll probably want to read them all, heh heh).

General

The Cambridge Field Guide to Prehistoric Life, *David Lambert*

Dinosaur, *Dr David Norman and Angela Milner* (Dorling Kindersley)

Dinosaur!, *Dr David Norman* (Boxtree)
Eyewitness Guides: Fossil, *Dr Paul Taylor*
Eyewitness Handbook: Fossils, *Cyril Walker and David Ward*
The Illustrated Encyclopedia of Dinosaurs, *Dr David Norman* (this is our favourite dinosaur book, not least because of its incredible illustrations by John Sibbick)

Specialist

The Dinosaur Heresies, *Robert Bakker*
Discovering Dinosaurs*, Mark Norell, Eugene Gaffney and Lowell Dingus*
The Macdonald Encyclopedia of Fossils, *Paolo Arduini and Giorgio Teruzzi*
The Riddle of the Dinosaur, *John Noble Wilford*
Tracking Dinosaurs, *Martin Lockley*
Wonderful Life – the Burgess Shale and the Nature of History, *Stephen Jay Gould*
Nature magazine
The Journal of Palaeontology magazine

Further watching

Ah come on, you know what the most essential watching for any dinosaur investigator is, surely? Yup, it's *Jurassic Park* and its sequel, *The Lost World*. While there is no possibility (yet) that scientists can re-create dinosaurs from DNA, these films are wonderful for their computer-generated re-creation of dinosaurs in all their glory. Of course, in the process of providing entertainment, some known facts are distorted –

Velociraptors were never anywhere like that large, for a start – but at worst any dinosaur fan can lean back and just marvel at seeing apparently real, living dinosaurs walking the Earth once more.

Unfortunately, there are few other films about dinosaurs that are worth watching. There are silly caveman-fighting-lizard epics like *One Million Years BC* and Japanese monster-stompers like *Godzilla*, but little of any real use to a dedicated investigator. Ever since King Kong had his punch-up with a large Tyrannosaur-esque dinosaur in the famous black-and-white epic in 1933, dinos have been misinterpreted and misrepresented in just about any film they appear in.

Thankfully, television will prove more useful in terms of programmes full of hard facts. Keep an eye open for documentary series and science magazine shows; these sometimes devote whole episodes to the latest finds from the world of palaeontology. Also keep an eye out for editions of shows like *Equinox*, *Horizon* and various specials on the Discovery Channel. Especially look out for re-runs of the wonderful television series *Dinosaur!*

On the other hand, try to avoid the television series *Dinosaurs* (you know, the one like *The Flintstones* but with rubber 'dinosaurs' walking about in clothes) and anything involving a large purple Tyrannosaur that sings songs and dances about. Yuck!

Further surfing

If you are lucky enough to have access to the Internet, you'll discover that it's a haven for enthusiasts and experts of all sorts. The Net's image as a free forum has made it an attractive place for the spreading of the craziest theories, so keep your eyes peeled for unusual answers to the Big Questions. More usefully, perhaps, also look out for appearances by well-known dinosaur hunters, whether answering questions in newsgroups or posing some of their own on university and museum home-pages.

World Wide Web

American Museum of Natural History:
http://www.amnh.org/Exhibition/Fossil_Halls/index.html

Carnegie Museum of Natural History:
http://www.clpgh.org/cmnh/vp/home.html

Dino Russ's Dinosaur Lair:
http://denr1.igis.uiuc.edu:/isgsroot/dinos/dinos_home.html

Dinosaur Egg Project:
http://www.infolane.com/infolane/apunix/dinoeggs.html

Dinosauria Online: http://www.dinosauria.com/

Dinosaurs at the Smithsonian:
http://photo2.si.edu/dino/dino.html

The Dinosaur Society: http://www.dinosociety.org/

Dinotrekking – the Ultimate Dinosaur Lover's Guide: http://www.bridge.net/~gryphon/dino/

Field Museum of Natural History, Chicago: http://www.bvis.uic.edu/museum/exhibits/dino/Triassic.html

Mighty Web Dinosaurs: Stick details of your own new discoveries here for the world to see. http://www.csd.net/~rsieg/dino/about.htm

Museum of Natural History, Stuttgart, Germany: http://ourworld.compuserve.com:80/ homepages/naturkundemuseum/homepage.htm

Natural History Museum, London: http://www.nhm.ac.uk/museum/lifegal/21/21.html

New Mexico Museum of Natural History – Dinosaur Footprint Page: http://www.aps.edu/htmlpages/footprints.html

T. Mike Keesey's Dinosaur Page: http://www.wam.umd.edu/~tmkeesey/dinosaur/ dinosaur.html

Terry Acomb's Dinosaur Tracks Page: http://www.uc.edu/~ACOMBTY/dinotracks.html

Virtual Museum – Palaeontology: http://www.exhibits.lsa.umich.edu/Virtual.Museum/

Newsgroups

sci.bio.palaeontology

sci.answers

sci.bio.evolution

sci.geo.geology

alt.dinosaur

alt.christnet.dinosaur

uk.education.expeditions

alt.books.crichton

Mailing list

The Dinosaur Society runs a mailing list that gives regular announcements of dinosaur events geared towards young investigators. To get their messages, you send them your email address and they send you their messages until you tell them to stop.

Send an email to listproc@usc.edu Keep the subject blank, but in the main body of the text write SUBSCR DINOSAUR [YOUR REAL NAME]. To stop, do the same thing but replace the first word of your message with UNSUB. More details are on their web pages.

Dinosaur Dictionary

Since palaeontology is a science which demands exact terms to avoid any possible confusion, it is riddled with thousands of difficult words and terms. We've tried to keep away from them, but there are always a few we just can't stop slipping in – so here's what they mean! For the meanings of more complicated terms than you can shake a Tyrannosaur's leg bone at, just go to your public library and look in the Reference section under 'Big Books on Dinosaurs for Stuffy Old Professors'.

Algae: Primitive water-dwelling plants

Ammonites: Extinct coiled shellfish found in great numbers

Amniote egg: Reptile's egg, that can be laid on land rather than in water like an amphibian's

Amphibians: Creatures able to live in water and on land

Anapsids: Group of reptiles including turtles and tortoises

Archosaurs: Major group of reptiles including the dinosaurs and pterosaurs, and living crocodiles

Arthropods: Animals with jointed legs, such as insects, spiders and crabs

Bipeds: Creatures that walk on two legs

Brachiopods: Sea-creatures with shells; they look like clams but aren't related

Cambrian: Ancient Period of Earth's history

Carnivores: Meat-eating creatures

Cast: A rock replica where a bone, etc., used to be

Cenozoic: Era from the decline of dinosaurs to the present day

Comparative anatomy: Guessing what an extinct creature was like by comparing it with a living one

Continental Drift: The movement of the landmasses over time

Coprolite: Fossilized droppings

Cretaceous: Period that saw the dominance of the dinosaurs

Deposit: An area of sedimentary rock

Diapsids: Group of reptiles including dinosaurs, crocodiles, lizards and snakes

Echinoderms: Sea-creatures, such as sea-urchins

Ectothermic: Cold-blooded

Endothermic: Warm-blooded

Erosion: Wearing away of rocks by the weather, water, etc.

Evolution: Gradual change in a species as it adapts to its environment

Exoskeleton: Hard outer casing of arthropods

Extinction: Death of every member of a species

Fossil: Preserved remains of a once-living creature

Fossil record: History of life on Earth as revealed by fossils

Gastroliths: Stones some animals eat to grind up food in their stomachs

Geology: The study of rocks

Gills: What fish use to breathe water rather than air

Herbivores: Plant-eating creatures

Ichnology: The study of trace fossils, including footprints

Invertebrates: Animals without a backbone (e.g. insect, crab, worm)

Iridium: Heavy metallic element found at the Earth's core and in meteorites

Jurassic: Second Period of the Mesozoic that saw the rise of the dinosaurs

Living fossil: Animal or plant species that's still the same today as it was millions of years ago

Mammal: Hair-covered creature; the mother feeds her young with her own milk (e.g. humans, dogs, cats, deer, mice)

Marsupial: Pouched creature similar to a mammal, mainly from Australia

Mesozoic: The Era when the dinosaurs walked the Earth

Mya: Millions of Years Ago; a measurement of time

Ornithischians: Dinosaurs with hip bones similar to those in modern birds

Osteoderms: Bones or bony plates that stick out of a dinosaur's skin

Palaeontology: The study of fossils; done by a palaeontologist

Palaeozoic: Ancient Era before the dinosaurs developed

Pangaea: Enormous supercontinent formed by Continental Drift in Permian times

Petrification: Turning to stone by minerals replacing soft tissue

Precambrian: Long period of time from the formation of the Earth until the arrival of life

Predators: Creatures that hunt and kill others

Pterosaurs: Flying creatures related to dinosaurs

Quadrupeds: Animals that walk on four legs

Reptiles: Leathery-skinned, egg-laying creatures such as crocodiles, snakes and extinct dinosaurs

Saurischian: One of the two groups of dinosaur, marked by elongated hip bones

Sedimentary rocks: Rocks formed by layering of material

Taphonomy: Study of how fossils are formed

Tertiary: Time from the decline of dinosaurs until the rise of humans

Trace fossil: Marks left by ancient creatures, such as tracks, scratches, etc.

Track: Series of footprints left by a creature such as a dinosaur

Triassic: First Period of the Mesozoic, before most dinosaurs arose

Vertebra: An individual bone from a creature's back

Vertebrates: Creatures with a backbone (fish, mammal, dinosaur, etc.)

Index

READ MORE IN PUFFIN

For children of all ages, Puffin represents quality and variety – the very best in publishing today around the world.

For complete information about books available from Puffin – and Penguin – and how to order them, contact us at the appropriate address below. Please note that for copyright reasons the selection of books varies from country to country.

On the worldwide web: www.puffin.co.uk

In the United Kingdom: Please write to *Dept. EP, Penguin Books Ltd, Bath Road, Harmondsworth, West Drayton, Middlesex UB7 0DA*

In the United States: Please write to *Consumer Sales, Penguin USA, P.O. Box 999, Dept. 17109, Bergenfield, New Jersey 07621-0120*. VISA and MasterCard holders call 1-800-253-6476 to order Penguin titles

In Canada: Please write to *Penguin Books Canada Ltd, 10 Alcorn Avenue, Suite 300, Toronto, Ontario M4V 3B2*

In Australia: Please write to *Penguin Books Australia Ltd, P.O. Box 257, Ringwood, Victoria 3134*

In New Zealand: Please write to *Penguin Books (NZ) Ltd, Private Bag 102902, North Shore Mail Centre, Auckland 10*

In India: Please write to *Penguin Books India Pvt Ltd, 706 Eros Apartments, 56 Nehru Place, New Delhi 110 019*

In the Netherlands: Please write to *Penguin Books Netherlands bv, Postbus 3507, NL-1001 AH Amsterdam*

In Germany: Please write to *Penguin Books Deutschland GmbH, Metzlerstrasse 26, 60594 Frankfurt am Main*

In Spain: Please write to *Penguin Books S. A., Bravo Murillo 19, 1° B, 28015 Madrid*

In Italy: Please write to *Penguin Italia s.r.l., Via Felice Casati 20, I–20124 Milano*

In France: Please write to *Penguin France S. A., 17 rue Lejeune, F–31000 Toulouse*

In Japan: Please write to *Penguin Books Japan, Ishikiribashi Building, 2–5–4, Suido, Bunkyo-ku, Tokyo 112*

In South Africa: Please write to *Longman Penguin Southern Africa (Pty) Ltd, Private Bag X08, Bertsham 2013*